For my beloved son, Zachary.

1

I step off the bus on the dusty Del Norte road, slip on my backpack, and turn to thank the driver.

"Take care, hon," he says. "Remember what I told you— get yourself some bear spray. Dash Bomb is the best."

They do this. Offer advice. Men. I must give off an air of helplessness or something. They think I can't take care of myself, but I can. I already have bear spray (I did the research. Raglan Defender is actually better so I got that one), not to mention the illegal riot-grade pepper spray I bought from an anti-rape campaigner on Craigslist. But I don't tell the bus driver any of this, instead I say, "Thank you, sir. I will."

He gives me a wink, levers shut the door, and carries on up the road. I watch the bus disappear around the bend and think, well, this is it, you're on your own now, let the fun begin. Amelia Kellaway. Adventurer. Woman alone. I do not plan on shaving my legs for months.

I take a breath. Pine. Soil. The barest hint of the sea. Straddling the road are dense woods of spruce and cedar. I look down at my feet and wonder where Oregon begins and California ends.

I think of Mom back in New York. When I told her I'd be gone for four months or thereabouts she said—

"I'd be happier if you checked in every week."

"That kinda defeats the purpose, Mom."

"Miss Independent."

"How come women are only ever called that—independent? Like feisty. I hate that."

"You know what I mean."

"Mom, I'll be fine. I'm the sensible one, remember."

She had looked at me and gnawed the inside of her cheek and I knew she was thinking she would be all alone because Danny was in the north, and Becca was in the south, and now me heading west.

Finally she placed a motherly hand on the crown of my head. "Okay, sweets, you go for it. Follow your dream."

Then she cried and blinked wet eyelashes at me. But I couldn't cry back because I was so happy to be free.

Across the road, there's a small Chevron and nothing else. I'm thinking it could be a good idea to use the bathroom before I start the trail because it might be the last civilized act I do. As I make my way over, I tell myself that I'm not procrastinating or afraid of the butterflies doing somersaults in my stomach. I'm up for this. The big adventure. I just need the bathroom first, that's all.

The gas station is a quaint, two-pump affair with a store attached. I'm almost expecting to see tumbleweeds somersault across the cracked concrete forecourt. There's only one car, not at the pumps but parked off to the side, over where people put air in their tires. Digging inside the trunk is a man, back turned from me. I think about calling hello but decide there's a risk I'll startle him and he'll end up smashing his head on the trunk lid.

I continue on and reach the store entrance. There's a sign in the window—a sheet of yellowed paper written with faded black permanent marker. *Restroom for paying customers only.* I open the door and go inside.

The day I left the employ of Winters, Coles and Partners was the best day of my life. They held a get-together in the top floor function room with million-dollar views of downtown Manhattan. My supervising partner, Alan, said a few words about how reliable and diligent I was, how I was always ready to jump in and pick up the slack, and how I once spent the entire weekend researching case law about the ecological impact on the New York wetlands. This helped Alan successfully argue against a last-minute injunction lodged by an environmental action group trying to prevent one of the firm's largest clients, the Hammond Group, from commencing construction on a multibillion-dollar development in the wetlands. Alan rounded out his farewell speech with an amusing anecdote about how I once inadvertently sent a confidential memo to the estranged wife of a client in a particularly acrimonious divorce proceeding. He quoted Proust. Then everyone ate cake.

But I knew about the water cooler gossip, how they discussed me with an eye-roll, how they said I was foolhardy to throw away a perfectly good career just to "find myself." They'd done the same thing when Melanie Barnes left the firm to buy a gelato cart and when Stuart Black turned his back on being a member of the litigation team to become a yoga instructor. I mean why study law and go through all those exams and bother sitting the bar and paying all that money and getting a student loan just to leave it all behind to pursue some half-baked pipe dream?

I knew some of them thought I'd be back in a week, that I was just going through a Gen Y phase thing and would see the light eventually, and return to the bosom of corporate life. A few of the others, like Ben Sinclair, told me privately they were envious and wished they had the guts to do the same—leave, go back to college to study theatre or film, or backpack their way through China.

But the rest thought I was just plain crazy, that Amelia, the obedient, diligent worker bee, had finally lost her mind.

But crazy was returning home to my apartment at three in the morning, drained and sick, living off canned tuna and ramen noodles because I was too tired to fix myself something proper to eat. Crazy was the marathon boardroom meetings and the backslapping WASPs who looked at my legs and cleavage and held open the door, not because they were being polite but because they wanted to show me my place. Crazy was walking in on Alan snorting coke off the cistern in the unisex toilet before a Supreme Court appearance. Sanity was realizing I had to get out before I went the same way.

Time was money and farewell get-togethers did not count toward billable hours, so my now former colleagues took their wedges of cake back to their battery hen cubicles, and copies of Black's Law Dictionary, and demanding clients, and half-finished briefs, and court dates, and filings of motions, and the endless hours burning the midnight oil all in the soulless pursuit of the almighty greenback bonus that I'd once coveted so much for myself.

After they had gone I stacked the dishwasher, took one final look at the glittering New York skyline, and walked out the firm's top-of-the-line, improbably large stained-glass doors.

*

I'm surprised when I go inside the gas station store because behind the counter I'm expecting to see an old-timer in denim overalls and instead there's a guy who looks a lot like Matthew stocking Marlboro Lights. I think maybe I should send Matthew a text, to let him know I've made it this far. But it has been over a month since we last spoke and it's probably better to let that particular dog lie.

On the left-hand side of the store, there's a carousel stand stocked with travel items like eye masks, plastic water showers, and compasses. On the wall next to it there's a corkboard pinned with hundreds of Polaroid photographs of trekkers, posing out front beneath the Chevron sign.

"It's tradition," says the guy at the counter. "Given we're the first stop."

He digs under the counter and pulls out an old Kodamatic. "You want me to shoot yours?"

I shake my head. "Thanks for the offer."

"You sure? I can take two. That way you'll have a copy."

I select a pack of spearmint gum and put it on the counter. "I'm good."

He puts the camera away and runs the gum through the till.

I hand over some coins. "Do you know where Clifford Kamp Memorial Park is?"

"Two miles up the road, you need to watch carefully for the access road. Which trail you doing?"

"The California Coastal."

He seems impressed. "Yeah?"

"From Del Norte to Mexico."

"That's a long way."

"Twelve hundred miles."

"By yourself?"

"Sure, why not?" I say.

"Most people start from south to north."

I shrug and he looks at me and I feel stupid because this guy isn't anything like Matthew at all.

*

The bathroom's outside and I punch in the 0000 code, duck inside, and take off the backpack. The toilet seat's cold but I'm not complaining because it's leaves for toilet paper from here on out. After I'm done, I face the sink and wash my hands, slathering pink goo between my fingers, washing and rinsing like a surgeon. Goodbye, running water. Goodbye, soap. Goodbye, last vestiges of my civilized life.

Nerves bubble in my chest. I'm not sure if it's fear or exhilaration or a mix of both. I laugh out loud. What the hell am I doing? I must be insane. Four months of camping outdoors, walking miles every day, fending for myself.

I look at the spotted mirror above the sink and reach for the pearl pendant around my neck, the pearl more purple than black, bought by Matthew for me on a trip to Hawaii. He said it looked good with my dark brown hair and olive skin. I roll it between my fingers then loop the chain over my head and hook it across the mirror. Maybe some other wilderness warrior will find it and make it her own.

I stare at my makeup free face, my clear eyes and skin, my cheeks blooming with roses. I smile. Let's get this show on the road.

2

When I cross the forecourt, I see the car again, an old time, pale green Ford Capri. Car buffs would call it a classic. The man is still rummaging through the trunk. There's a jack on the ground next to the rear left-hand tire. A pair of crutches leans upright against the bumper.

"God darn it!" The man lifts his head from the trunk. "Oh, I'm sorry. I didn't realize I had company."

He's in his late forties with sun-kissed skin, broad-shouldered and tall, dressed in blue jeans and a T-shirt. Bordering on cowboy or salt of the earth. He has friendly eyes.

"No offense," I say.

"I got myself a flat and this—" He hops a few steps back and points to a moonboot on his right foot. "The universe hates me."

"Bummer."

He nods to my backpack. "You off on vacation?"

I stand a little straighter. "More journey than vacation. The California Coastal."

"Yeah? You doing the whole thing by yourself?"

"Why does everyone keep saying that?" I joke.

He shrugs. "I think it's neat."

"I'm stronger than I look. I once fought off an addict who tried to snatch my purse."

"I bet." He frowns. "Let me guess—New York?"

"That obvious?"

"You'd be surprised at how many East Coasters we get here." He winces and clutches his thigh. "For the love of Christ, I'm having no end of problems with this thing."

"What happened?"

"You'll laugh," he says, crow's-feet fanning.

"I won't."

"My boy and I were working on a tree house in our yard, and good old Pops here fell right off the ladder and landed on his fanny."

That's sweet, I think, a tree house. I always wanted one of those. I try to ignore the flash of my own substandard childhood.

"Did I say something?" he says, looking concerned.

I plant a smile on my lips. "Not at all."

I look up at the blue sky and realize I'm employing delaying tactics again.

"I should go."

"Foolish really," he says, "falling like that. It wasn't even that high up."

I glance at the road. "It was nice talking to you."

He nods. "Sure. Take care."

"You too, sir."

He disappears back into the trunk and I turn for the road.

"Mother of Christ!"

I pivot around. He's dropped the jack and is stretching for it.

"What the heck was I thinking?" I say. "Let me help you."

He points to the flat near his feet. "Would you give me a hand to put this in the trunk? I keep losing my balance."

"Of course."

So I pick up the flat and place it in the trunk and just like that, it's over. He's so quick, lassoing his arm around my shoulders, pressing the rag to my face, so quick that I barely register what's happening before my limbs go hot then numb, and I watch, in a rapidly descending fog, as the wooden crutches clatter to the ground and he hauls me inside the trunk, pushing me in there, pushing me on to my side so I and my backpack will fit, pushing down hard on my back with both hands, the way you might stuff too many clothes in a suitcase. I feel the sharp edge of a plastic tarp on my cheek, the grit on the back of my head, an unidentifiable object jabbing my thigh, then before I get a chance to scream the steely underside of the trunk lid hurtles toward me and the lights go out with a thump.

3

Matthew was supposed to come with me on the Coastal. On our third date, I told him about my plans. It had been reckless of me, but we'd been walking through Central Park and dogs were chasing Frisbees and the sun was streaming through the maples and a girl with purple dreadlocks was playing a banjo. When Matthew took a bite of his pretzel, wiped the corner of his mouth with his thumb, and asked me if I wanted any, I said—

"I'm going off grid."

"Yeah?"

"Just for a while."

"That's brave," he said, picking a sesame seed from his teeth.

"You could come."

He'd traveled a bit before. Europe. South America. Now he was trying to make a name for himself in mergers and acquisitions. But he was disillusioned, too. The grind, the way they used you up and spat you out. He finished his pretzel and said he would give it some thought.

I had planned my escape from Winters, Coles and Partners for nearly two years. I spent hours on the Internet, researching. Bought guidebooks. Read blogs. Watched *National Geographic*. All I knew was I wanted to be someplace else. I wanted to move my body like it was meant to move, and not be cooped up in some office cubicle day after day.

I imagined myself as a great explorer, criss-crossing continents, taking in the sights and sounds of the

Australian outback, Peru, Great Wall of China, or something closer to home, like the Rockies or the Californian Coastal trail.

I began to collect things. Stake out camping stores on the weekend. I bought a flashlight that worked by kinetic energy so you didn't need batteries, a compass, wet wipes, water purification tablets, a whistle, earplugs, a heavy-duty Swiss army knife, a polyester super quick-dry towel, insect repellent, carabiners, a top of the line Condor backpack.

The nights when I couldn't sleep because of the stressful, coffee-fueled days in the boardroom, I would take the backpack from its place on the top of the wardrobe and lay out everything on my bed, filling every square inch of it until it looked like an army surplus store. I would gaze at those shiny, useful objects and tell myself you can do this, you need only make the call, write that letter of resignation. But by morning, when the sun rose over the city, I would put the things away and return to the big office in the sky and push any thought of leaving to the back of my mind. Then I met Matthew and Matthew called me brave.

I'd seen him at the welcome when he first joined the firm. Our eyes met across the apricot pastries and lemon brioche and he smiled. He looked vulnerable, standing there in his new suit, collar tight around his neck, as his supervising partner introduced him to everyone. I later found out that blue tie with the tiny maroon hexagons was a gift from his sister.

He made love like a Greek god, would put his heart and soul into it, gaze into my eyes with an intensity that reminded me of glass in the sun. Afterward, he would fold me up in his arms like a father.

We exchanged "I love yous" on a rare weekend away. One of the partners, Chip Emmerson, gave us the keys to his vacation house in the Hamptons, which was actually more mansion than summer house. Matthew and I had gone from room to room, astonished at the scale of the place, marveling at the furnishings, Hellman-Chang everything. Looking up at the Rothko hanging above the Italian marble staircase, Matthew had uttered, "God, one day we could live like this."

We made love in the pool house because the main residence was too overwhelming. Lying there on the cotton blanket in the afterglow, I murmured into his shoulder—

"Why don't you come with me?"

"Where?"

"To do the Coastal."

"I would follow you to the ends of the earth, you know that," he said.

"I'm serious."

"So am I. Let's do it," he said.

"Truly?"

"Truly."

The weekend was cut short when Chip Emmerson arrived unannounced, and he and Matthew spent the rest of the weekend discussing futures and the downfall of the latest Madoffesque scheme, but that was okay because Matthew had said yes.

4

The shudder of the car wakes me. My brain is syrup. My eyelids lead. I inch them open. There's something on my face, a cloth, tied at the back of my head, my hair caught in the knot. The cloth covers my entire face like a mask, and is ripped open around my lips. I can smell its newness, the plastic sheath it had lived in when it sat on a shelf in some Walmart or Target. It could be a dish cloth or bandanna or pillow case. Whatever it is, it's cheap and nasty and like sandpaper against my skin.

I'm lying on my side in the backseat of a car, hands tied behind my back. They are secured so tight I can feel my pulse thump from one wrist to the next. My feet are tied, too, the knobs of my ankles jammed together.

The fabric of the mask is so poorly constructed that when I turn my head the right way I can see through the open weave. In the driver's seat there's a man. He sits on a wood-beaded seat cover, hand draped over the steering wheel, eyes on the highway. We are moving along asphalt, smooth and undulating. I hear a car whoosh by, the back draft of a big rig, the drone of a motorcycle.

Something catches my eye. Hanging from the rearview is a small Kermit the Frog. Like you would get on a key chain, made of cloth, with matchstick-thin gangly legs and splayed out feet. I watch Kermit dangle there, lobbing from side to side, and begin to think I must be trapped in some crazy dream, that I've been slipped acid in a club, or had some type of seizure.

The cogs of my mind turn slowly, straining to put things together. The man looks familiar. I have seen him before. But it's so hard to think. Then it comes to me. The gas station. The moonboot. The flat tire. I nearly laugh out loud because this must be some kind of joke. A prank of epic proportions. He was so nice, so ordinary, there can be no other explanation.

But what's that on my lips? Blood? And what else, Amelia? The ties and the mask? It comes back in a rush, being rendered unconscious and thrown into the trunk of his car.

"What do you want? Why are you doing this?" I say, surprised by the fact that I'm slurring. "You have to let me go."

He shoots a look over his shoulder, lifts his brass-rimmed aviators, then pulls sharply to the side of the road. Somewhere in my fogged up head I know I've screwed up.

He opens the door and gets out and I hear the slow, steady crunch of his boots as he circles the car. He's watching me, I can feel it. He's outside the left rear window, his body blocking the light.

A car passes and after it's gone, he opens the door and pauses again. He reaches inside and touches the top of my head. His whole hand settles there, like a human skull cap, and I do my best not to scream.

I think that maybe I should say something—If you let me go now, I won't tell anybody. I don't know who you are so I'll never be able to identify you. My father is a law enforcement officer (he isn't) and he'll be out looking for me as we speak so give this up before you make matters worse for yourself.

"I have money," I say.

"Do you?"

"You can have all of it if you let me go."

But it doesn't matter because here he comes with a rag and the chloroform or whatever it is, leaning in, unhurried, putting his knee on the seat, holding the rag over the gash where my mouth is, and before I know it, I'm gone again.

5

It's dark when I wake. My head is pounding. And the thirst, the thirst is unbearable. The car's not moving and I'm alone inside it. I angle my head and find a strip of light, unnatural and fluorescent. The smell and noise of gasoline shuddering into the tank.

Outside, voices. Faraway and indistinct. I lift my head. Through the tiny squares of cloth, I see him, hands on his hips, talking, unhurried, to the guy at the adjoining pump. The gasoline stops chugging and he removes the fuel dispenser, shuts the flap with a snap, and goes inside to pay.

Even in my groggy, drugged up state, I know I should do something, that this may be my one and only chance. Then it dawns on me that he has made a mistake. Despite Moonboot's plan to incapacitate me with zip ties and blindfolds, he's forgotten the gag. So I shout. I shout as loud as I can.

"Help! Somebody help!" I kick the door with my feet. I'm overjoyed because it's thunderous—the banging, my voice. Someone will hear for sure. "Help! I'm in here! My name is Amelia Kellaway and I've been kidnapped! Call the police!"

The door flies open. Oh, thank God.

"I've been kidnapped," I say breathlessly, "from a gas station on the Oregon-California border. You've got to help me."

I try to sit up but am shoved back down again. My head is pinned to the seat.

"Well, would you look at that—a fighter."

It can't be. There are people here. They have to come. They have to see what's happening to me.

Before I can yell again, something is forced into my mouth, and a blanket, heavy with the fresh scent of Ultra Tide, is pulled up over my head. I struggle against my bindings, try to make noise, but it's no use. Moonboot simply shuts the door and drives away.

*

The next time I stir I've wet myself. I can smell it. Not strong but there. My shorts and underwear stick to my skin. It's pitch black and I can't see a thing through the tiny squares. It's impossibly still and I wonder if I've been moved someplace else, a basement, an attic, a shed in the woods.

I listen hard for clues. Night crickets. The lone hoot of an owl. The swish of tall grass. A faint, cool breeze through an open window. I deduce I'm still in the backseat of the car. Moonboot is sleeping. I can hear the curl of his breath. He's reclined his seat all the way back and it's pushing against my lower legs.

He mutters something and shifts his body, projecting wet snores in my direction. For a moment, I think he might be fake-sleeping and watching me instead.

I start to cry. I don't want to. I don't want him to win. But everything hurts—my head, my wrists, my arms, even the mere act of blinking in this stupid mask. I tell myself, don't give up, you can't give up, you will get out of this nightmare.

*

17

"You messed yourself."

His voice shatters my blissful void of sleep.

"My bad," he continues. "Next time let me know and we'll work something out."

It's the first time he's spoken a full sentence since he took me. The way he talks, he could be your next door neighbor or the guy on the bus.

We are driving again. And it's light. The morning kind. The quality of the air has changed, too. There are shadows of buildings, small-town noises, a lawn mower, a jackhammer, cars, the sluggish forge of a train. I wonder how many miles I am from Del Norte.

"We got to make a stop, fighter. So I'm going to ask you to behave for a bit, if that's okay with you."

Keeping the engine idling, he pulls over, reaches into the backseat, pushes a rag in my mouth, and covers me with that blanket again. He drives a few more feet, takes a sharp right. A disembodied voice crackles through a drive-thru speaker.

"Welcome to Wicked Joe's Burgers, what can I get you?"

Moonboot gives his order and collects his food. He drives for ten minutes and parks up somewhere quiet.

He dislodges my gag, removes the blanket, and settles down to eat. I can see him through the gauze of my mask, staring out the windshield as he chews and sucks on his straw. I watch his jaw rotate and begin to salivate from the smell of bacon and sausage and cheese and ketchup.

Abruptly, he leans and pokes the straw into my mouth. "Wet your whistle with that."

I nearly vomit at the thought this straw has also touched his lips but I drink and the tepid orange juice is wonderful and the glucose floods my bloodstream and I feel instantly giddy. Next he pushes an egg-soaked corner of a bun into my mouth, followed by a wedge of sausage patty and more juice.

He smashes the trash into a ball and lobs it in the garbage bin outside. I listen to the metal flap swing back and forth and think DNA. Our DNA. Mixed together on that straw and how no one will ever know this important piece of evidence is there.

I'm expecting the chloroform again, but it doesn't come. Instead, he says—

"Settle in, fighter. There's a long drive ahead."

6

Matthew and I never actually talked about when we would go. I was content enough to live off the fantasy, the two of us out there in the windswept wilderness, sharing aluminum pouches of freeze-dried food, making love under the stars. It was like oxygen to me.

The dream kept me going through the long days and nights at the firm when I would sit in those torturous marathon meetings and imagine the sun on my shoulders. I started buying items for him from my little supply shop on Lafayette Street. Soon I had two of everything. Pocket lights and compasses and mini binoculars and waterproof ponchos. I splurged and bought a double sleeping bag for couples.

One day I suggested we set a date and work toward it and he didn't object. I chose late August. The tail end of summer. The days would be bright but not too hot. Ideal conditions for daytime trekking and nighttime snuggles.

Then "The Deal" happened. It was all he could talk about. *The Cooper Deal.* It was worth eighty million dollars and a huge bonus for him. He and the partners and sycophants would disappear into the war room for days. Matthew slept under his suit jacket at the office, lived on coffee and bagels. He started to tent his fingers and stroke his tie and slap backs and use expressions like "synergy" and "value-add" and "sea change."

"It's such a rush, Amelia, to be part of something this big. These guys, man, I can smell the money coming out their pores."

I told myself it was the lack of sleep, the adrenaline, the poor nutritional choices talking, not my free-spirited, anti-capitalist Matthew.

But it only got worse. He was always wired, talking a million miles an hour, tense like a coiled spring. Sometimes he looked right through me. Even the way he made love changed. It was like he was engaging in some sort of sport, grunting and grinding. Ejaculating was scoring a touchdown. Everything had become a game.

The Cooper Deal was followed by the Sampson Deal and the Carter Deal and the Heller Van Asch Deal and Matthew seemed to slip further and further out of my reach until one day I walked in on him screwing Melissa, the shiny new intern, on the sofa in the breakout room on a Friday night. I stood there, momentarily transfixed by the two glinting nipple piercings on Melissa's swinging breasts, then simply walked away.

I didn't wish Matthew any malice or bear him any grudge. I knew it was the machine, chewing him up, spitting him out, affecting his brain, the way he thought. It was like a disease.

I only hoped he would survive it. Because one day there would be a crash, whether it was him or the corporate scheming, and he would face the ledge of despair, or the noose, or the taste of a gun, because that's what happens to good men. Good men fall while bad men thrive.

7

On the floorboard I can make out a dog collar with tags, the green leather tip worn and split. I wonder what the dog's name is, whether it's friendly or vicious, where it is now. I like dogs and have always thought highly of the people who owned them. Clearly I would need to change that assessment.

The effects of the stupefying solvent were lessening and my thinking was getting clearer. I tell myself that I must log details, for later, for when I escape. Ten things. Just focus on ten things.

First my surroundings. The car. Mint-colored Capri. Wood-beaded driver's seat cover. Kermit the Frog on the rearview. In the center dash, reusable coffee cup encased in a purple rubber rim with a Hawkins oil refinery logo on it. Squeaky spring under my left hip. Striped mocha-colored upholstery. Everything shiny and pungent from Armor All. No trash, apart from a single fluttering receipt on the floorboard next to the dog collar.

I wonder if Moonboot is one of those guys who vacuums and waxes his car every Sunday, if he has a house without a thing out of place, if he likes everything just so and flies into a rage at the slightest sign of dust. Strangely, it's more worrying that he isn't a slob. You'd expect someone who abducts a woman from a parking lot in broad daylight to be a rambling, disorganized nut job. Moonboot is none of these things. He is different. Confident. Together. Maybe even smart.

I glance at the receipt and I'm thinking it would be a big help down the road to show what he bought, the time he bought it, the store he bought it from. Maybe it would lead to a name on a credit card or a face on a camera. But if I reach for it now he will undoubtedly see, so I bide my time and decide to wait until later when I get a chance.

Then there's him. I tilt my head and squint through the mask to study his profile. He has a good nose, not too large or small, but perfectly proportioned. Strong jaw line, brown hair graying at the temples, so he is probably older than I initially thought. Early fifties, skin the color of nutmeg. Muscular, as if he works the land, healthy, except for his mind, there's nothing healthy about that. His movements convey a casual self-assurance, like he is in control, like he knows he will not get caught, like he's done this before.

I shut my eyes and test myself. Like the game I used to play as a kid with my brother, when Mom would put a selection of items on a tray and we had to memorize as many as we could before Mom finished counting to five and covered the objects back up again. Then my brother and I would scribble furiously for twenty seconds writing down everything we could remember. I always won, which would infuriate my brother and send him stomping off to his room.

In law school I honed my technique and used a trick to help me recall the hundreds of cases I needed to know for exams. I would make up little stories. *Marbury v Maloney* was Maloney on his owny. *Doyle v Ohio* was Doyle shot Mike Loyal. The trick was to picture an actual scene like a movie. Maloney on his own in a playground as a kid because his mother had abandoned him. Doyle at home drinking with his friends before an altercation with his irate, meth-addicted friend, Mike Loyal. It worked like a charm. Even now, ten years later, I can still recall the mailbox rules off the top of my head. And there's a story here, for sure, a vivid nightmare of a story that I won't forget soon. This time the lead character isn't Maloney or Doyle, it's me.

*

It feels like we are heading north. It's difficult to tell because we've been driving for what seems like days, in different directions. But north is my best guess, north into Oregon, maybe even as far as Washington State.

There's a change in the air. It gets fresher. Goosebumps strike along my bare thighs. The sun seems further away. The sounds are different too, closer. No longer the open spaces of fields but something else. I angle my head back. Trees—tall, substantial, the smell of pine.

We leave the sealed road and I feel roughness beneath the tires. The suspension screeches and gravel pings.

Moonboot clatters inside the glove box. A few moments later the stereo bursts into life. Neil Young. Jimi Hendrix. Johnny Cash.

It looks like Moonboot is stuck in the dark ages and hasn't heard of an iPod or Bluetooth because the music is on a cassette tape and being played on what is probably the original Capri car stereo. A homemade mix tape, spliced together. The songs have been recorded directly off the radio. I can tell because of the awkward transitions, the accidental clunk of the pause button before the song has ended properly, the clumsy manner the DJ has been edited out.

There are eight songs on side one, and seven and a half on side two. As we circle the rough terrain, Moonboot lets the tape play over and over. He is apparently a Johnny Cash fan because there are four Johnny songs in total, more than any of the others. I think of Joaquin Phoenix thumbing that band saw and Reese Witherspoon in her June Carter dress and the day I was shocked to see the real Johnny Cash on MTV, bloated and pockmarked and ancient, singing a cover of a Nine Inch Nails song, "Hurt." I think about how I wept because by that time June Carter was dead and Johnny looked like he was very near the end himself. It was one of the saddest things I'd ever seen— this once great, diabetes-riddled old man singing about how hurt he was, the saddest thing, perhaps, other than being kidnapped from a gas station and tied up for days in the backseat of a car by a lunatic who had a liking for classic rock and Kermit the Frog.

8

I need the bathroom again. But I don't want to ask. I don't want his pity. I don't want his favors. So I just go. Warm fluid seeps between my thighs and I experience a tiny burst of satisfaction that I am peeing all over his precious, mocha-colored upholstery. Then I think that maybe if I can make myself as filthy as I can he won't touch me. But that would mean number twos, and I can't bring myself to do that. Not yet, anyway.

My body is feeling the effects of being stationary for so long. The tendons in my shoulders are screaming. My arms ache from being tied behind my back. Both legs are in permanent cramp. The cloth mask has become like a second face and, perversely, I'm beginning to find comfort in it. Like a child in a living room tent made out of bed sheets. It gives me a sense of privacy, a distance between him and me.

We snake around the road. I feel the pull of gravity as we go uphill. Loose items roll inside the trunk. A hazy memory comes to me. He put me there originally, that first day at the Chevron, into the trunk. Then I get worried because I don't remember how I got from the trunk to the backseat. Whole snatches of time are blank. Did he do something to me that I don't know about?

The thought of him touching me when I was unconscious makes me sick, but there's no way to tell because my clothes are intact. Then I start thinking that eventually we're going to stop and eventually he's going to want something from me—sex, violence, my life. But before I go further down that road, I stop myself. For now I'm alive and uninjured and lucid. Like my mother used to say—one raisin at a time, Amelia Jane.

*

He turns on the headlights. I know this because there's an audible hum, like an old tube TV warming up. I can also see the blue glow of the dash. The Capri corkscrews up the mountain, because that's what it is by now, a mountain, and my body rolls hard against the backseat and my ears pop and I feel oh so carsick. Just when I think I might throw up, the terrain flattens out and we are circling back down the other side.

About halfway Led Zeppelin begins to slur. Moonboot jabs a button and tries to remove the cassette tape but the ribbon is caught and he tugs and the tape unspools and the car swerves, then swerves back as he corrects the steering, and he finally gets it all out and tosses the empty cassette on the empty passenger seat in a cloud of ribbon. I think that this might make him angry, especially if it's a favorite mix tape, but he doesn't seem bothered.

Instead he declares, "That's it, fighter, we're here."

And the car rolls to a stop.

9

I used to think my father was the smartest man in the world. When I was little I would find him in his attic study, glasses perched on his nose, pouring over rolls of technical drawings. He was an engineer. He designed bridges and was known for inventing a new kind of strut called the Beverly Strut (named after my mother) which helped bridges avoid collapsing during earthquakes. He had this little model of the Golden Gate Bridge on his side table. He'd frown whenever I touched it.

He was always in his study working with his rulers and protractors and pens and charts. I knew it was important that he get it right, that cars and buses and motorcycles and people crossed bridges every day and they had to be safe.

Sometimes if I hung around long enough, he would give me a sheet of paper and a pencil and show me how to draw a simple plan for a birdhouse or go-cart or jewelry box. When I became too much of a pest, my mother would arrive and usher me out. *Your father needs to work now, Amelia Jane, give him some peace and quiet.* When I'd protest, he'd reach into the tin of fruit candies he kept in his top drawer and drop one into my palm and tell me he'd come and play later. I would go outside in the backyard and wait on the swing set or ride my bike around the yard with my brother. Sometimes I would look up at the study window and see my father standing there staring at us, smoking the cigarettes he wasn't supposed to smoke.

I didn't know it then but he wasn't interested in bridges anymore. He was planning his escape, visualizing a new future, a different life without us. Then one day he left and never came back.

I used to ask my mother if he left because of me and she would say through wobbling lips that my father loved me very much and that nothing was my fault. I didn't believe her because when my father was at work I would sneak up the stairs into his study and spin in his squeaking chair and pretend to smoke and mess about with the Golden Gate Bridge. He found out and didn't like it and he left.

10

The car stops and Moonboot turns and looks at me for the longest time.

Finally, I break the silence. "I won't say anything if you let me go."

It's laughable. I know this when I say it, but it's all I've got.

"Won't you?" he says.

I can't tell if he's angry or amused or just indifferent.

He stares at me awhile longer then gets out and opens the passenger door and lifts off the blanket and cuts the ties to my ankles and the pulse returns to my legs.

"Get up."

My heart beats wildly because I know this is bad, this is the reason for the long journey, the blindfold, Johnny Cash.

"Do as you're told," he commands when I don't move.

I sit up.

"What's your name, sir?" I say, reaching.

"Stop talking."

"I was spelling bee champion in the third grade and voted most likely to succeed in sixth grade. I love animals and banana splits and my grandmother. I had my first kiss when I was twelve and collected for the blind foundation and one day I want kids. One of each. Or both the same, I don't care as long as they have ten fingers and ten toes."

I've gone too far because his hand grips my upper arm like a vise. He swivels me around so I'm sitting on the edge of the seat and takes off my boots.

"Walk," he announces, lifting me up by the elbow.

"You won't get away with this. My husband will be out looking for me right now. I'm a lawyer. You're going to go to prison for a very long time. Unless you let me go. Let me go and I won't tell anyone. Before things go too far. Think about it. I don't know who you are. You could just leave me here and simply drive away. I can find my own way back."

He pushes me along. Pine needles and stones prick the soles of my feet. I can't see much through the mask because it's dark apart from the headlight beams.

"My name is Amelia."

"Lie down."

"Amelia Jane Kellaway."

I think how dumb it was to tell him my full name because now he will probably hunt down my family and kill them.

"I said lie down."

I break loose and run. My body has taken over my mind and I run. I cannot stop it. The situation is terrifying, the way my body is moving without my consent, like I'm a mere bystander to my own life, and I want to stop because it hurts like a roller coaster, that choke of terror at your throat, the oxygen that's just out of reach.

He's behind me, too close, boots thumping, breath heaving. He is running fast for a man of his size. I can see myself from above, with this stupid rag-mask on my face, hands tied, barefooted, careering into trees, the shadow of him gaining ground.

Think like a champion, I tell myself. Visualize success. Me first at the finishing line, getting that hole in one, making the hundred-yard touchdown. I see myself getting away, finding a road, flagging down a passing car, ripping the mask from my face to look out the back window at the figure of him getting smaller.

I trip. Face first. My knee cracks against a rock and I scream into something that might be moss. I try to quiet myself, to bear the pain in silence, lie as still as can be because there's a chance I've fallen into some sort of valley or ditch and he can't see me.

I wait. Seconds. Minutes. Nothing. There might be hope.

"I don't blame you, Amelia Jane Kellaway. I would've tried, too."

He's standing above me like a monolith. I wonder if he's been there the whole time.

"Cooperate and you live," he states.

I start to cry and hate myself. "*Please.*"

"Say yes, Amelia, and you live."

I'm crying hard now. It's so difficult to breathe with this rag on my face, and I know what I'm in for, what he wants, I can hear it in his voice, smell it coming out his pores.

He kneels down and gets close. "Say it."

"Oh God."

"Do you want to live?"

"Yes, I want to live."

He does it right there with his knees in the water.

11

I wake up warm. Through the tiny squares of the mask I see flames from a campfire. I don't know how long it's been since the river, an hour or two maybe, but it must be late. It burns between my legs. I think about the act of war committed against my body. I should feel some emotion but I only feel numb.

"Hungry, Amelia?"

He is somewhere to my left. There's the clash of metal on metal as if he's eating from a can. When I don't reply, he tries again, softens his voice like a concerned friend.

"Come on, Amelia, you've got to eat."

There's a clunk as he puts down the can. He shifts toward me and pulls me up to a sitting position with his powerful hands.

"Here you go," he says. "Give this a try."

I feel something cold on my lips. Spam. I eat even though I want to throw up because I don't want to give him an excuse to exert his power again. He puts the neck of a water bottle to my lips and I gulp that down too.

"Tastes okay, doesn't it?" he says, spooning in more Spam. "A fraction down home but it hits the spot, wouldn't you say, Amelia?"

He leans back on his heels, waiting for an answer, so I nod.

"Good for you, Amelia Kellaway," he says.

He resumes feeding me as if I'm a child. I can see him through the cloth. His face is lit by the fire and set in a pleasant paternal expression. He has an incisor snaggletooth and a scar on his chin. He has changed into a dark green and crimson checkered flannel shirt, creases ironed to perfection, brilliant white crew neck T-shirt beneath it.

Abruptly, he stops. He lowers the fork and stares at me. He comes close, so close, in fact, that I can smell the pork on his breath. He waves a hand in front of my face.

I shut my eyes and tell myself to be still. I can't let him know I can see him. It's the one advantage I have.

He wipes the knuckles of his hand against his jaw as he thinks.

"Okay," he says, sitting back, satisfied.

I rearrange my legs to let out some tension and he moves to the other side of the fire and stokes the embers with a stick, throws on more wood. Then he is out of my line of sight, going to the car, popping the trunk.

For one God awful minute, I think he's going to make me sleep in there. But then he's back by my side with that blanket, kneeling down to slip a zip tie around my ankle, securing it to his own so we are Siamese twins. My skin itches at the thought of being next to him all night long or that he may touch me again, accidentally or otherwise. To my relief, he keeps his distance and lies on his back with his arm under his head.

"Would you look at those stars," he says.

He pulls the blanket up so that it covers our shoulders. I catch the scent of leather polish and salt and freshly laundered clothes.

"Sleep tight, Amelia."

*

34

I feel a tug on my leg. It's Matthew rousing me for one of our rare Sunday morning brunches at that sweet little diner near Central Park, the one with the best eggs Benedict and freshly squeezed pomegranate juice, and a great window seat where you can watch little kids skip their way to the zoo. But when I open my eyes, I see the porous weave of the cloth, and remember exactly where I am.

It's daylight. The forest is alive with morning sounds. I see his outline, half-turned from me, putting the zip tie he's taken from our ankles into his jacket pocket. He stands, stretches, and looks over his shoulder.

"Morning," he says.

He kicks the ashes of the dead fire with his boot.

"You like coffee? Of course you like coffee. Who doesn't like coffee?"

I pretend I'm asleep while he retrieves a large bottle of water and tips some into a metal container then puts the container on the small gas cooker to boil. He opens a cooler, gets out two plastic mugs, and spoons in some instant coffee, pouring in hot water last.

He looms over me.

"Sit up." I don't move. "Quit fooling, Amelia. I know you're awake. You've got coffee coming."

I give in and try to raise myself up but it's difficult with the zip ties on my wrists so he helps me to a sitting position and guides the mug into my hands.

"Don't burn yourself."

I think about throwing it in his face. Then what? Run again? Make him angrier than before? So I go with it and take a sip. It's piping hot and way too strong.

He makes oatmeal in the metal container and feeds me again.

35

"Do your hands hurt? Your wrists?"

I nod.

"It needs be one or the other." He sounds apologetic as he removes the wrist ties but secures my ankles.

After he's done, he stands up and rubs the back of his neck.

"Okay," he says, blowing out a breath. Like, okay, there's work to be done. Okay, what can I do to her next?

Okay turns out to mean performing the mundane duties of cleaning the breakfast bowls and coffee mugs then returning to the trunk to pull out a shovel and two brown tarps. He lays one tarp flat on the ground between two trees, and hooks three tartan bungee cords through the other tarp's aluminum grommets and secures it to the tree like some sort of lean-to shelter. He retrieves something else. A sleeping bag and two pillows.

Oh God. I've seen enough true crime documentaries to know how this goes. He's in this for the long haul. He carries on, busies himself gathering wood, setting up the supplies, digging a latrine, and I lie down on my side and close my eyes because I don't know what else to do. I can tell by his light-footedness that he's happy and I wouldn't be surprised if he started humming or whistling to himself. I try to think of a plan, some sort of plan, to regain some control, but I seem to be in this strange state of shock, a stunned paralysis of the mind where everything will not compute properly, as if I'm a survivor of a plane wreck, walking around in circles in my own mind.

12

When he shakes me awake again, it's dark. I've slept for the entire day. He tries to give me a polystyrene cup of instant noodles but I push them away.

"Come on, now, Amelia."

"I don't want any," I say.

He pauses and puts the noodles on the ground. I feel him come close and I flinch because it makes me think of yesterday when he touched me and I'm not sure I can survive a second time. His forearms brush against my ears and I brace myself and wonder if he's about to push my head down into his lap. I think to myself that I'm going to bite that sorry thing off but he unties the knot of the mask instead, releasing the cloth from my face, taking great care to arrange the hair around my shoulders.

It's a shock to see him, unfiltered and larger than life, so close, looking at me with his caper green eyes, jaw rotating while his molars crush what's left of his food. All I can think of is Kevin Costner in his older years. A man's man. A broad-shouldered man's man in a tavern with a misted mug of beer in his big fist, shooting the breeze with the burnished-skinned old-timers, recounting a day of felling trees or hunting or building a barn from scratch. A man's man who, for some reason, wanted me or someone like me—a proxy for a mother or sister or aunt he blamed for some deep-seated wrong done.

Slowly, he strokes his chin as he studies me. Then, quite suddenly, he says—

"You have pretty earlobes, Amelia Kellaway. Very pretty earlobes. I like the fact they're not pierced."

He picks up the noodles and holds them out. "I know things must be strange for you and what-not, but it's important you eat, Amelia. Just a few forkfuls, would you do that for me?"

I hear his words but I'm still in shock that he's removed the mask.

"Amelia?"

I nod my head.

A smile breaks out on his lips. "That's the spirit."

He reaches around and runs a strand of my hair through his forefinger and thumb. I wonder if he has a "type" and whether I fit it. I wonder if any woman in her late twenties around five-seven with medium length-brown hair is enough to turn his head and cause him to strap his leg into the moonboot and pull the flat tire routine. I wonder if I am simply one of a number, and if I am, what happened to the others.

He moves to the other side of the fire and lounges against a tree trunk, one shoulder against it, watching me. I pick up the noodles and bring the tiny plastic fork to my lips. I attempt to still my shaking hand and wonder whether this is the moment I should beg for my life.

"I need the bathroom," I say.

He looks at me and pauses. "You bet."

He removes the ankle ties and pulls me to my feet and walks me to the edge of the campsite and points to the hole in the ground he dug earlier.

I'm free and this is my big chance to run but I just stand there.

"Go on," he says.

I squat over the makeshift latrine, balancing my right foot on one side, my left on the other, and deliver the whole shebang. It all comes out, everything, and I'm mortified by the noise and the smell. I glance up and he's turned his face away, averting his eyes. I need to wipe myself and he gives me a roll of toilet paper then turns his back again.

"It won't always be like this," he says.

*

He has a large bag of Honeycrisp apples. He has already eaten two and is on to his third. He offered me one, but I told him my stomach hurt, and after the latrine, he doesn't push the issue.

"You don't say much, do you?" he says, chomping.

He's emanating a syrupy aroma and I know I will never be able to eat my mom's apple pie again.

He pulls my backpack toward him, opens it, and begins rifling through. I feel instantly violated with him going through my things like that, pulling out my tees and sweats and underpants and sports bras. He finds my copy of *Anna Karenina*, the one that I thought would double as entertainment and a bug killer.

"Tolstoy," he says, spitting out a black pip. "I'm impressed. Although I prefer Steinbeck myself, but then I guess I've always been a patriot."

He puts down *Anna* and continues searching. He finds my wallet and opens it.

"So you weren't fooling about being a lawyer," he says, studying my business card. "Manhattan, no less. Your parents must be proud, Amelia."

I wince and he sees it.

"I touched a nerve." He stares me. "Issues with your folks? I understand. My mother was no better than a street whore herself."

He returns the card and pulls out the photo of Matthew that I was planning on using in a farewell-to-ex-fire-lighting ceremony somewhere along the trek.

"And who's this? Hubby?" He studies the photo again. "No, not hubby. He's a stopgap, a fly-by-nighter, Amelia. I know his type. I can tell just by looking at him that he's not for you."

As he's returning it to the wallet, he finds the other photograph. Veined and crumpled. Me as a two-year-old on my father's knee taken out the back of our house, the house later foreclosed on by the bank after he left.

"Oh, this is sweet."

"Put it back," I say.

He stares at me. "You were close to your pop."

"I said put it back."

"You're right. I apologize, Amelia," he says, returning the photograph. "We don't have to talk about it."

He hurls the apple core into the brush and takes out his own wallet.

"Since were sharing—"

He shows me a photograph of a boy about six standing next to a black BMX.

"That's Noah," he says, face darkening. "He's older now, thirteen. I get emails sometimes. He's stayed strong, despite his mother's lies. She was never my wife, just a waitress, a nobody. You look like her but I won't hold that against you."

He touches the photo. "I wear my heart on my sleeve, I know that, but when it comes to Noah I can't help it. I sure miss him a lot."

He takes a final look then returns the photo to his wallet and falls silent, staring morosely into the fire.

Finally, he lifts his head and looks at me.

"I'm sorry, Amelia. About before, about what occurred at the river, it won't happen again."

He's so earnest I almost believe him.

13

Rightly or wrongly, his words have given me hope. If he says he won't touch me again, maybe there is a scrap of humanity in there. Maybe I can reason with him. Maybe I can gain his trust.

So when he asks me if I want to go fishing I say, "Yes, sir," and try for a smile. He nods, happy, and says, "That's just swell."

He laces up my boots and we set off, my wrist secured to his, weaving through the towering pines, between narrow openings, up and down the undulating terrain. All around there's the shriek of unseen birds, the shuffle of hurried, retreating steps. The vastness of the place is overwhelming. I know that if I was to zoom out, then zoom out again, we would be nothing, mere arthropods in the undergrowth. I want to reach out and touch everything—the bark, the soil, the sticky pungent sap. Scrape the ground until I fill my fingernails. Roll the fallen leaves against my cheeks. I glimpse myself as I was meant to be—the trekker, fresh-faced and eager, at one with nature.

"Turn left here."

We go into deeper, thicker woods, and I begin to worry I've miscalculated his intentions and I'm actually walking to my death. We carry on and follow a path between the trees and I keep my eyes out for landmarks, any sign of a road that I can return to later, but it all looks the same.

He takes me past thickets, up to a ridge, then we circle back down to emerge on the other side to face a lake as smooth as glass.

"Beautiful, isn't it?" he says, laying the fishing rod on the ground.

I can't deny it. It's more than beautiful. The picture book lake is bordered with elegant maples dripping fall-ripened leaves into the water. Water lilies float in clusters on top. But the most spectacular thing is the water itself—it is the most dazzling shade of crystal blue I have ever seen.

"There's a spring down there. If you dive deep enough you can actually feel it bubble up from the rock bed aquifers."

After leading me to the riverbank, he undoes the wrist tie, rolls out a blanket, and sits me down. He slips out of his jacket and hangs it on the hook of a tree branch. There's a gun tucked in the back of his belt. He turns to me.

"Ever fish?" he says.

I shake my head. "No, sir, I haven't."

"You're in for a treat then. How about it? What to give it a try? Say yes."

He's playing with me. I can see his eyes dancing.

I nod. "Sure. Thanks."

He puts the rod in my hands. I think hard about how I can use it as a weapon but decide to stick with my original plan of befriending him. He circles me and I avoid cringing when his body engulfs mine. He clamps his hands on my wrists and swings the line back and forth in powerful strokes, the stones of his biceps flexing against my arms.

The bright red feather lure lands in the center of the lake.

"Oh, you're good at this, Amelia," he says.

I think of his son, Noah, and wonder if he ever stood where I am standing, with his father's voice in his ear, telling him what a great job he was doing.

I hold the rod on my own, the line ballooning in the breeze, that gaudy red feather lure so out of place among the rest of the surroundings. Moonboot crouches to wash his face in the water, lifts his cap, and runs some over his head. He stands and looks out at the lake.

"This is what the world needs to get back to, Amelia," he says, "simplicity. Taking only what you need. No commercial production. No profit-driven culture. Think how much happier the world would be without Wall Street and multi-national corporations and bankers and lawyers. I feel nothing but pity for those people. They'll never experience real happiness, not like this. Feeling the wind on their faces, the earth between their fingers, tasting meat caught with their own hands. But you know what I'm talking about. You were part of it. All of that lust."

"I wasn't," I say it before I can stop myself.

"No? You sure? You didn't want a pair of those Jimmy Choos whats-its? I bet you pressed your nose against that polished glass and imagined slipping your pretty toes into that soft baby calf leather to send a signal to the world that Amelia Kellaway had finally made it."

"You don't know anything about me."

And he didn't because for me it was never about the money or status or accumulating meaningless material things. For me it was about accomplishment, proving myself, quelling that corrosive sense of not being quite good enough.

Moonboot stares at me. "You're right, Amelia. I apologize. You're not like them. I know that. That's why I chose you."

I shudder but try to rise above it and remind myself that I'm supposed to be gaining his trust.

"Do you mind if I ask your name?" I say.

He looks at me for a long time and does the thing when he lifts his forefinger to rub the spot just above his top lip.

"It's okay, forget I asked, it's none of my business." I say.

"Rex."

It's his real name, I just know it, and I feel violently ill. Why couldn't he have just made something up? Not only do I know his face, but now also his name, and he doesn't seem to give a hoot. Don't go down that road, I tell myself. Keep him talking. Get him to let down his guard.

"What do you do for a living, Rex?"

"Chatterbox today, aren't we?" He pauses. "Take a guess, Amelia. What do you think? Doctor? Lawyer? Candlestick maker?"

"I don't know. I can't see you in an office. You work on the land?"

He seems pleased with my answer. "In a manner of speaking," he says, but before he can elaborate he shouts and points at the water. "You got a bite!"

A sudden tug on the line. Then another. The rod bends so much that I think it will snap.

"Pull back," says Rex. "Gently now, Amelia. You want to snag him, make sure that hook gets good and stuck in his cheek before reeling in."

The water ripples in circles and the line is so taut I'm sure it has snagged a rock. The line jolts again.

"That's it, Amelia. Bring it up. Slowly, now. Slowly."

The fish is fighting. The reel is whirring.

"Wind it, quickly, that's it."

The fish breaks the surface and dances on its tail. I reel furiously and bring the fish in to the riverbank. Rex unhooks the flapping creature and lays it on the plastic bag.

"I did it," I say, exhilarated. "I really caught a fish."

*

He roasts the brown trout in foil over the fire. He allows me the first bite, flaking off the milky white flesh into my bowl. It tastes good and fresh and real. Not like the thrice-crumbed grocery store fish that has been minced with God knows what else and shaped to look like a fish. We eat until there's nothing left except a wide-toothed comb.

"I'll wash up, Amelia," he says. "It's only fair."

He tosses the bones into the flames and scrapes and washes the plates. When he's done he sits down and stares at the fire.

"I'm going to let you go," he says. I look at him to see if he's joking. "Take you back so you can carry on with whatever you were going to do."

"Now?"

He lifts his eyes to the forest.

"It's too close to nightfall. Tomorrow."

14

I sleep in fits and starts. Is he playing me? Stringing me along in some twisted mind game? The desperate part of me wants fiercely to believe that I have managed to humanize myself enough for him to release me. It happens, doesn't it? There are entire true-crime series made about survivors of terrible crime who live to tell the tale. Yes, I say inwardly, that's it. Think positive. Send out those optimistic vibrations to the universe—believe it and it will manifest.

By first light I'm fully awake but he's still asleep beside me. I wait, watching his passive face inches from my own, and tell myself this is the last time I will be tethered. Tonight I will be sleeping in a bed, an actual bed, on my own.

He stirs and opens his eyes.

"Morning," I say an octave higher than usual.

He blinks at me and says nothing and for one horrible moment I think he's going to rape me again. I mean, why wouldn't he? Once hardly makes the trip worthwhile, does it? He knows I won't resist, that I won't risk him not letting me go. But he breaks off eye contact and sits up.

"I don't know about you, Amelia, but I need coffee," he says, clapping his big hands together.

I nod. "Yes, coffee would be good."

As usual, coffee is followed by porridge and him washing the dishes and putting them away. When he's done, he turns to me.

"Let's get you cleaned up before we hit the road."

I want to tell him I don't need a bath. I can live with myself. Even though I stink worse than week-old trash. But it's a good sign. He probably just wants to get rid of any trace of his DNA on my body before he lets me go.

We take the hour-long hike to the lake and once there, he digs inside his duffel bag, hands me soap, and points to the water.

"In you go. I won't look. I'll sit right over here."

He does what he says and settles down on a log, facing the opposite direction. Quickly I undress and dip into the water, which is breathtakingly cold but fresh. I put my head under, wet my hair, scrub my face.

"Finish up now, Amelia," I hear him call. "There's clean clothes in the bag."

I splash soap from my face and check that his back is turned then hurry from the water naked. Inside the bag I find a fluffy white towel and a brand new summer dress made from expensive cloth. It's embossed with exquisite daisies and comes complete with a $150 price tag. It's chilling, I think, the extent to which he has thought this through—the moonboot, the tire, the camp in the woods, the dress meant for his perfect size four victim. Trying not to think too hard about it, I slip the thing over my head, and when I go to remove the tag, I see that it's secured with a tiny safety pin. Something tells me to hold on to it, so I do, attaching it to the underside of my hem where it can't be seen.

"Put your old clothes in the bag when you're done."

I comply and stuff my fancy high-priced trekking gear into the bag and tell him I'm finished.

He turns around and nods his approval.

"Suits you," he says, walking over.

He fills the duffel bag with rocks and tosses it into the lake.

"Let's go."

But "let's go" doesn't mean let's go back to civilization and the gas station where this entire sorry mess started, it means let's go back to camp so he can work on his car for the next three hours while I sit holding my breath. It means checking and filing every one of the Capri's four spark plugs, disconnecting and removing the battery so he can examine, clean, and oil the carburetor and four other critical parts. It means getting on the ground and sliding on his back under the chassis to adjust the front and rear axles and check the tread on the tires and an apparent hole in the muffler.

I tell myself to be patient, that there's still time to leave before nightfall, that he's just making sure the car can handle the journey back into town. But morning light changes to afternoon light then to dusk. Finally he stops what he's doing and closes the hood and throws me a tin of spam.

"Eat that."

He turns away and soaks a rag in turpentine, uses it to wipe grease from his hands. I think to myself, okay, this is better, something to eat and we'll get going. I peel open the can and eat. Rex is lingering over by the tarp lean-to drinking a bottle of water.

"Aren't you going to have any?" I say.

He shakes his head. "I'm good."

"Is the car fixed now? Are we going soon?" I say, between mouthfuls.

49

He doesn't answer and heads for the box of supplies instead. He pulls out the longhead matches and fire starters.

I put down my can of Spam. "What are you doing? We don't need a fire. We've got to get going."

He won't look at me.

"What are you doing?"

"Tomorrow," he says, without lifting his eyes.

He criss-crosses the kindling and places three fire starter cubes on top.

"Tomorrow? What do you mean tomorrow? You said we would go today."

He strikes a longhead match and ignites the fire starters.

I get to my feet.

"Sit down," he says.

"We're leaving today," I stammer. "Now."

He doesn't move.

"You said we would."

"Sit down, Amelia."

I am shaking with anger. "You need to let me go."

"I said tomorrow."

"I don't believe you," I say.

"Suit yourself."

"You were never going to let me go." I bunch my fists. "You're a liar."

"Sticks and stones, Amelia."

I move closer.

"You belong in an institution," I say.

He tosses four logs onto the fire. "Probably."

"No wonder you're all alone."

"That's quite a tongue you've got there," he says.

"No wonder your wife won't let you see your son. Do you even have a son? Or did you just make that up?"

"Of course I do."

"He probably hates you."

Rex lunges for me. "Hush now! I don't want to hear another word out of that nasty mouth." He shakes me hard. "Is that clear, Amelia? We go when I say we go."

He pushes me to the ground and stomps off to the edge of the camp, stands there with his back turned, hands on his hips.

"You can't keep me out here forever," I say, finally.

He looks over his shoulder at me. "That's exactly what I intend to do."

15

When I was eleven, I found a dead cat in the bushes behind the apartment complex we moved to after my father left. The poor thing had snagged its collar on a nail near the top of the fence and hanged itself. I ran inside to tell my mother and she hugged me and told me it was all right to be sad.

She was going to put the stiff little corpse out in the trash but I insisted we bury it in a shoebox under a holly bush. For weeks after, I would go there and lie on my back on the grass and talk to the holly bush cat. I would tell it about my day, the test I aced, how Nathan Krabbe put gum in my hair, and how Daisy Walker, my apparent best friend, dumped me for Kathy Carter because Kathy had a pair of Doc Martens leather boots and I didn't. Then one day a work crew arrived and began removing the holly bush and shredding the surrounding trees and laying asphalt. I watched powerless as a giant roller pressed the steaming tarmac into place, and the guy in the Construction Worx T-shirt painted out a parking grid with a little machine on wheels right over the spot where the holly bush cat lay.

I turn on my side and think of the cat and how its owner never knew what happened to it. I think of my mother and her little barky lapdog, Jed, and how she will never know what happened to me.

I feel like an idiot for believing him. Like a susceptible pensioner lured into a Nigerian scam. Matthew always said I was too trusting.

Rex has barely spoken a word in the two days since he refused to take me back. He performs his daily tasks in a perfunctory, distant manner, furrow chiseled into his brow—wake up, remove the zip ties, make coffee, eat breakfast, clean camp, do not engage with the prisoner. In the afternoon, he might collect and chop firewood, venture out to lay some animal traps, take care of the latrine, but there was no talking to me.

I watch all this from the sidelines, where I have withdrawn into my shell, lost in a deep depression I can't fight my way out of. The days seem long and gray and hopeless. The only bright thing is the leaves from the maples and aspens which seemed to have turned red and gold overnight.

This afternoon he returns to camp with two dead raccoons swinging from a length of twine. He's brighter than usual and announces that tonight there will be stew. He plants himself on an upturned bucket and deftly skins, guts, and dismembers one of the unfortunate creatures, placing the parts in the saucepan, adding water, and simmering it over a low heat. He strings up the other raccoon on a branch near me and leaves it there, and those unblinking black eyes fix on me in a thousand-yard stare.

Somewhere close to dusk, the stew is ready. He gives me a plateful and takes one for himself, and digs in heartily. I have no appetite and I pick at mine, hoping he won't notice.

"Something wrong with your meal, Amelia?"

"No."

I try harder and close my eyes and imagine my mother's Sunday roast and manage to finish the plate. Once dinner is over, he turns to me and places both hands on his thighs.

"Ready?" he says.

By this he means toilet. He's religious about taking me to the latrine four times a day on a very precise schedule—7 a.m., 11 a.m., 3 p.m., 7 p.m. Like a pet in a kennel, I have learned to go on command.

He leads me across the campsite to the pit, which is remarkably odor free even though we have been using it for days. He has some sort of system in place, where he covers it a little after every use with a mixture of dirt and lime.

He does his usual back-turning thing and I crouch and notice the cool metal of the safety pin brush against my thigh. An idea comes to me. Secretly I unclip the pin and pierce my thigh and smear blood on my fingers.

"I've got my period."

He turns around. "What do you mean?"

"I'm menstruating." I show him my bloody hand. "Do you have anything?"

By the look on his face, it's clear he hasn't thought this far ahead.

"Tampons? Sanitary pads?" I say.

He shakes his head and for the first time he looks unsure of himself. "No."

"A cloth then?"

"Of course, Amelia. I'll find something. Wait here."

He heads for the car and disappears behind the tree line.

Now's my chance. A minute at the most to put as much distance between him and me before he realizes I'm gone. I scan the forest. Which way should I go? It all looks the same. It doesn't matter. *Go. Go now before he comes back.*

I choose left and dash for the trees, my legs rubber with adrenaline, my bare feet quickly shredded to bits.

Behind me, he's calling my name. I run and run headlong into darkness. Branches whip my face, tear my cotton dress. I go further in, circling around bushes, pushing through the brambles, ignoring my screaming feet. It's so dark, so deep.

He's not far behind, crashing through the undergrowth, steps heavy with outrage.

I veer left and now I'm running down the track to the lake. If I can just get to the lake I can swim across. Suddenly it appears before me, shining like a pearl. I clamber down the bank and get ready to launch myself into the water but I slip on a greasy rock and my foot slides out from beneath me. And here he is, thrashing through the water, grabbing my ankle, pulling me back. I try to break free with a kick, but he hauls me up and shakes me like a doll.

"Why did you do that!"

He drags me up the bank and back to the campsite by my wrist.

"Stay there!" he says, pushing me to the ground.

I'm a dripping mess and so is he, hair plastered to his head, clothes sodden. The cords on his neck are pumping and I'm crazy with fear because he's never been this angry. He begins to pack up the campsite. Folds the tarps, rolls the sleeping bag, puts the trash into a plastic bag, pours water over the embers, buries the latrine.

I begin to blabber. "Don't worry, I'll never say a word, and I understand you're just going through a rough patch, we've all had those, and I know you're not a bad person, that you only wanted some company, and I don't mind, truly I don't, all this, it'll stay between you and me, and in fact, I'm grateful because this whole experience has taught me something valuable, that my life is precious, yours too, your son's as well."

The campsite is empty and he glances around for a final check.

"And now we can get on with our lives. Each begin anew. This is just a blip, that's all, a blip. Just drop me on the side of the road. I'll walk, hitch a ride, whatever. You don't need to go out of your way. It'll be as easy as that."

He looks at me. There's a different face now.

"Shut up, you fucking bitch."

He takes three great strides and knocks me out cold.

*

When I come to I'm in the trunk of his car. He's driving too fast for the rough terrain and the car fishtails and the brakes squeal. He barrels on regardless, taking the next bend too aggressively, causing the car to slide again. I wonder if his plan is to drive off a cliff and kill us both. All I can think about is how I'm going to be a Saturday night mystery, and how my body will never be found, and how my mother will rock back and forth on the front porch at night and look at the stars and wonder where I am. There will be yellow ribbons tied to mailboxes and tree trunks and then first-year, then two-year, then five-year anniversaries. I will be a cold case in a manila folder in a dusty archive box in the bowels of a county police station. At my high school reunion they will speculate on my disappearance. There will be rumors that I ran off to Spain with a married man. I will be reduced to the phrase "Whatever happened to Amelia Jane Kellaway?"

I wish there was a way I could leave a message, scratch a goodbye note to my family, but I can't feel my fingers even if there was somewhere to write.

The car stops sharply. He gets out. There's the squeal of the back door opening, followed by his retreating steps. I wait and wait. Listening for anything, trying to temper my halting breath. Then the trunk swings open and he's back, pulling me over his shoulder, carrying me a few feet then dropping me to the ground next to a grave-sized hole.

"God no."

"Get on your knees."

His face is glistening with sweat and blackened with dirt.

"Wait. You don't need to do this."

"I said get on your knees."

I do as he commands and start to cry. "Please don't do this," I sob.

"Say my name," he says.

"I'm sorry."

"Say it."

"I won't run again. You have my word. I made a mistake."

"Say it."

"Rex."

"Again."

"Rex."

He kneels down in front of me and puts his hands around my throat.

"Just remember, Amelia, I gave you a chance."

"No, no, no, no."

He squeezes, his eyes laser focused, lips rigid. I claw at his hands. I am fading, slipping in and out, the world

graying at the edges, and I can only think of one thing—
how the hands on my throat once held a newborn.

Wilderness

16

Before my father left we lived in a big house in a good part of town in Ithaca, New York, called Redmont. The house was a picture-perfect, two-story American Colonial with navy blue shutters. It had a farm-style kitchen, six bedrooms, and a large rose garden. Out of all the rooms he could have chosen for his study, my father selected the smallest room, located in the attic. There were places in that room where he couldn't stand up straight because of the pitch of the ceiling. I'm not sure why he chose it, whether he had a thing for confined spaces or simply because it was the most silent area in the house. I used to think that maybe it was so he could watch and wave at us kids when we played in our yard.

The house had a name—Redmont Rose. My mother invented it. She even had the name etched into a plaque made of walnut and hung it just above the doorbell so everyone would know what the house was called. Our yard bordered a huge park, with streams and a fort and a freshwater lake with ducks and swans. My brother and sister and I treated it like an extension of our yard and used a secret hatchway in our fence to go back and forth.

Every year the neighborhood held cookouts and summer picnics there. But best of all were the Fourth of July fireworks extravaganzas put on by the Lions Club, who flew in a specialist team of pyrotechnicians from Sweden to run the event. Once my father took me to the top of our garage roof, promising it would provide the best vantage point to watch the fireworks over the lake. I remember looking at his face, luminous in the pink glitter of an exploding horsetail, and thinking how much my six-year-old brother looked like him. When the fireworks ended, I didn't want to get down but eventually he convinced me that we would come back next year and do it again. Then he returned to his study and his technical drawings and worksheets and I was corralled into another room by my mother so he could get back to work.

Six months after my father left, my mother had to sell our beautiful house. She was very brave. She piled us into the station wagon and told us not to look back, that our new place—an apartment, an hour's drive across the other side of town—was just as good, *if not better*. She actually said that. It wasn't. I had to double up in a tiny room with my sister, while my brother slept in what was meant to be a utility cupboard under the stairs.

What my mother didn't know was that every Fourth of July I would return to our old house in Redmont and sit on the garage roof to watch the fireworks. One day the man who was living there nearly caught me so I ran off and never went back.

17

At first I think I'm dead. It's the black. The absence of sound and air. I feel cheated because I want the white light, the outstretched hand of dear Nana May. Then I realize I'm not dead after all. There's dirt in my mouth and nose, choking me, pinning me down. And it hits me. Oh God, I'm suffocating. Someone help. For the love of God, someone help me. I hear a voice—my own, Nana May's, God's—I don't know whose but it's telling me to move. *Hurry. Think fast. Get out.*

A sharp object presses against my right knee, a stone or stick, so I focus on that, moving my knee. Left, right, left, right. It's taking too long. My lungs scream for oxygen. My head's about to explode. I try harder. Pivot my leg back and forth. But there's just no way.

My brain turns to cotton and I begin to fade. Somewhere in this fuzz, I think of him—his face, his hands around my throat, the whites of his eyes. What he did to me. I won't allow him to win. I push with everything I have, press my ribcage against the load, arch my back. But the dirt might as well be a solid wall.

I try to remember every bad thing I ever saw, the YouTube clip of that white supremacist pouring Jim Beam down a puppy's throat, that time in eighth grade when Brent Maxwell stole the cowboy hat from the Down Syndrome kid on the way to school in the bus, those people in the Twin Towers who had only two choices— burn alive or jump. It works. Adrenaline jets into my veins. I thump my chest against the earth tomb and a small channel opens up and I can scarcely believe it and I think more angry thoughts and fight harder and dirt loosens and crumbles and finally gives way and I go up and up until I'm breaking through the surface and sucking in the wet night air.

I begin to laugh. I did it. I am free. I am alive.

I brush the soil from my face and blink into the dark and my joy fades. He could be here, watching on in amusement, ready to do it all over again. I listen for his breath, the snap of a twig, the sound of his voice. I lift myself out of the grave and force one jellified leg in front of the other, heading for the trees, moving quickly but carefully to avoid knocking myself out on the low-lying branches. It's so dark I can't see my own hand in front of my face.

I reach the first spruce and pause there and listen again. I keep going, arms out front as I walk, changing course whenever my fingertips brush against bark or the sharp point of a branch.

Swallowing hurts. I try not to think about it, that someone tried to kill me, but I can't help it. I walk and cry, sputtering into my hands because I don't want to make a sound in case he's still here, and, oh God, trying not to cry, trying to hold it in hurts my throat and I wonder if there are broken bones in there or if he's fractured my windpipe because this aching doesn't feel normal and I think to myself this is trauma, I am traumatized, I am split in two—the before and the after.

I drop to the ground. I try to get up but my feeble legs give way.

I look at the forest. The blackness is impenetrable. All around me, pines creak. Things scamper in the undergrowth. The distant moan of a wolf.

I back up against a tree and stay there, listening.

Something comes near. The crack of timber. Slow, careful steps. I cannot breathe.

I reach out and feel the ground beside me. A rock.

I take a shallow breath and taste iron on my lips. A pinecone comes loose and drops into the leaves. Then nothing. I press myself close into the bony roots of the evergreen and remain there with the rock in my hand. My human scent engulfs me. I wait and listen in the long, dark night.

18

Sleep does not come. The night inches by. Finally, light begins to seep through the treetops. With it, patches of brilliant blue. The forest stirs in ways different than before. Cicadas rasp. Birds flit overhead. A bunch of sagging oxeye daisies stiffen in the sun.

I look around. I am in thick, steep woods. Even so, I feel exposed. Is he here? Hidden where I can't see him?

He's gone, I tell myself. I have to believe that or I will be paralyzed with fear.

I spit out some dirty drool and glance down at my filthy skin, the black bruises around my wrists and ankles, my bare feet. I'm trembling from cold and shock. Move, I think.

I stand up and face the woods.

"Okay, I got this."

But I remain anchored to the spot and before I know it I'm sobbing again. Last night someone tried to kill me. Last night I nearly died. I wring my hands and cry in breathless waves. I am a weak, bewildered child. I bang my head with my fists. Cut it out. Don't go crazy. You can't afford to go crazy. Go crazy and you're as good as dead.

I take a deep breath. *Focus. Select a direction. Walk. That's it.*

I begin to calm down. Yes, I can do that. I wipe my face and look at the forest. All I need is the road he took to get in here. It can't be far—I didn't cover that much ground last night.

I choose right and move forward into the wilderness, which is like a fairground illusion that just keeps going. Pines, and spruce, and other trees that could be cedar and oak molt gold and copper leaves. Fall has come early. Soon the nights will be cold.

I tell myself that doesn't matter because a day or two at the most and this nightmare will be over. I will be out of here, clasping a hot drink, foil blanket around my shoulders, telling the police everything I know. The ten things. Kermit the Frog. I will tell them about that and the army blanket and the mint Capri and the brass-rimmed aviators. And him. Rex. His face. It's right here. I'll never forget it. His kid's too, the boy in that dog-eared photograph standing next to a black BMX in his white sports socks. I hope he won't grow up to be like his father. I hope he won't hate me for sending his daddy to prison because that's exactly what I intend to do. It hits me then—I never got the license plate. How could I be so stupid? I search my befuddled brain. Maybe an O, K, 1, and a 7, but that's it.

I walk all morning long, my bare feet cringing against the hard earth ground braided with roots and rock. I ignore the pain and trudge through the forest, searching for any sign of the road. But there are just trees and more trees.

The poles of spruce sway and creak high above my head and I lick my roughened lips and think of the water I don't have but desperately need. I wonder how long a person can live without it, and whether I will just keep on shrinking until my body dries up like an onion skin left out in the sun. This makes me think of my mother, the sun worshipper, who would coat herself in baby oil until her flesh was as glossy as a Danish, then starfish on the concrete out in back of our tiny apartment for hours on end. My mother and those ugly watercolors she used to make and the paint-spattered Monet T-shirt she wore for a nightgown. Then I think of my father and how all of us waited night after night for him to come back.

Morning dissolves into midday then afternoon and there's no hint of the road or the grave. I rest on a boulder and listen to the wind whistle through the trees. It all looks the same and I can't be sure which way I've come. I chide myself for not having some sort of system. Marking trees as I went. Leaving a trail.

I wipe the debris from the soles of my feet, get up, and walk on.

I reach a slope with a series of switchbacks, pathways long overgrown, most likely belonging to an old packhorse trail. I stop and do a 360. There was none of this last night when I ran from my grave, I would have remembered.

But the switchbacks could lead to a hill allowing a better vantage point so I carry on, skirting them as best I can to avoid the brambles and what could be poison ivy. Back and forth I go, zigzagging upward, but the pathways only lead me into deeper, thicker woods.

I step in mud, then a puddle. I kneel down and scoop the brackish water into my mouth and wash my face. Sitting back on my heels, I look at the tiny pool. Branching out from the puddle is a trickle, just a ribbon really, and I wonder whether I should follow it. It could lead to a tributary then maybe a river or lake, and hikers or campers.

I continue on and track the water and it soon grows into a creek large enough to step into and soothe my feet. Every so often, I stop to ladle some into my mouth, and tell myself I mustn't forget to do this—I can live without food for a while but not without water.

The ground becomes impassible, overrun with thistles, goosegrass, and gorse, and I'm forced to circle back down and leave the creek behind in the hope I can rejoin it on the other side. I weave through a swatch of trees, over some rocky hillocks, and hear the trickle again. I follow the sound until I see the glistening crack. But the creek is no more than a dribble now, and when I walk ten more yards, it dries up to nothing.

Fatigue overwhelms me and I lower myself onto a fallen log.

I have lost all sense of time. I can't tell if light is fading or if the dimness is just because I am so low in the valley. For all I know, evening could be about to drop.

I pull a splinter from my left foot and watch a kernel of blood appear. I think of the red feather lure. Then him. I think about how stupid I am. For all of it. Believing I could do the trek in the first place, for lifting that God damn tire into that trunk, for being naive and trusting and just plain dumb.

I haul myself up and walk on. The light is deserting me, and I try not to think about how I will have to spend another night in the growing cold, without food, clean water, proper clothes, and with animals I cannot see. My body cries out for rest, especially the soles of my feet, which are being pummeled by the stony terrain. But there's no choice. I have to keep going.

I ascend the slope, breaking a sweat, my arms two dead weights by my side. I pray the terrain will level out soon but it only gets steeper. Breathless, I wipe perspiration from my eyes and look over my shoulder. Dense woods are way behind me and I'm surprised to see how far up I've climbed. I face front and carry on until I'm stopped by a large cluster of rocks. This could be good, I think. Beyond the rocks there may be a summit.

Digging deep, I search out toeholds and places for my hands to grip, hoisting myself up a little at a time. My arms scream for me to stop but I keep going, and with one final push I crest the highest boulder and step out onto a ridge, where I'm rocked by a sudden, frenzied wind. That's when I see, in a blink, how much trouble I'm in.

19

In the bleak, graying light, nothing but trees and hills for miles in every direction. No highway. No town. No tracks. Just woods. In the far distance, scree slopes and jagged, snowcapped peaks. All I can do is blink at the infinite landscape with my wind-dried eyes, not knowing what else to do.

A moonless black drops like a sheet and finally the dark and cold force me to move. Stumbling across to the other side of the ridge, I feel my way down a grassless slope until I am out of the wind. I take shelter in a gully of rocks and sit shivering, knees pulled up to my chest, back pressed into the iron-cold stone.

I am nothing in this sheer vastness. A mere seed in a canyon. How am I ever going to get out of this place? And what if he is here watching and lying in wait? No, I think, he's returned home, slipping back into his mundane everyday world, reliving memories of my life slipping away in his hands. As far as he's concerned I am dead and buried and no longer a problem.

There are nighttime noises again. Coming close, then backing away. Hairs on my arms stiffen. Thoughts become a jumble. My foot itches. I can't let myself fall asleep. Whatever is out there could get me. *Stay awake. Remain upright. Count the stars.*

The night crawls by. With my hands tucked into the pleats of my armpits, I listen to the constant hiss of the wind, my chattering teeth, the wailing wolves. I think of my old life. It wasn't so bad, was it? There were clean sheets, mattresses, pillows, hot baths, Starbucks double shots and Supreme King burritos. How nice the Manhattan skyline would look right now, that spectacular view from my partner's office I took for granted, the smoked fish canapés and Australian red wine, and all that mingling with corporate clients. Matthew.

Don't go there, I tell myself. Don't go to the Mexican restaurant we loved so much, and our hand-in-hand walks through Central Park past the guys on the bongo drums, and making love on a Sunday afternoon as the sun blessed us through the window. Don't do it. Don't look back.

By daybreak my head feels like it could slip from my shoulders and I know I can't not sleep forever. But for now I return to the ridge. Sky the color of seawater hangs over the vast land. The beauty is not lost on me. Heaven, or some part of it, will surely look like this.

Tracking the frosted clouds as they drift east, I study the terrain. Four choices. North—mountains. East—flat land covered with thick trees. West—more mountains and fields of scree. South—the trees thin out, a small hill, possibly a clearing and grassland, the glint of a waterway and what looks like a gorge and maybe a bridge. This could mean farmland. From up here it's too hard to tell, and I don't know anything about distances, how many miles it would be to get there, just that it seems very far away.

But I can't stay here and south could mean people.

Before I leave I use tiny pebbles to spell out my name and my mother's phone number beneath a giant SOS, and the words—*Alive. Gone south.*

All day long I weave my way through the assembly of trees, pausing frequently to scratch and inspect the underside of my troubling foot. I think about how cruel it was for him to take my shoes. Then I remember that it didn't happen that way. I ran from him and he caught me and killed me and I came back to life. I tell myself that I mustn't forget. The ten things, especially. Mint Capri. Kermit. Beaded seat cover. Boy on a bike. O, K, 1, and 7.

As I walk I think of my life, my childhood, my worst and best mistakes. I think of my mother.

"Talk to me, Amelia, I'm worried about you." This was her refrain from my childhood. Her other favorite was "Sweets, it's not good to bottle things up. You need to let them out."

My mother is a verbalizer, the type of person who feels the need to announce every single thing that pops into her mind. What's worse, she has no filter. Announcing things I think best kept private.

Like the times I'd hear her on the phone to her friends. Amelia got her first period today. Amelia had a bad case of diarrhea after camp and messed her pants. Amelia cries herself to sleep at night.

I never felt the need to share everything I did or felt, so whenever my mother said, "What's going on in that head of yours?" I would tell her that everything was fine. "There's nothing to talk about, Mom. I just need to get on with my homework."

She didn't even know I'd broken up with Matthew.

I know what she's going to think when I don't come back. She's going to think I ran off. She'll tell everyone I needed space, that I was more fragile than anyone ever knew. I think of how broken-hearted she's going to be. What's worse, she will blame herself. My poor mother, the woman who desperately tried to hold her fracturing family together after my father left.

Oh, how I wish she was here now. With a needle and a Band-Aid and some antiseptic cream for this irksome foot. My mother liked nothing more than to lance a boil. She once said she must have been a nurse in a former life.

*

Late morning and I breach the tree line and step into a field of astonishing yellow. Stretching out across the clearing, thousands of wild mustard plants convulse in the strong northerly wind. Bees levitate over the blossoms, their hind legs inked with gold. I bend to pluck a mustard flower, crushing it between my forefinger and thumb to rouse the spice. My nose itches and I toss the bud away and lift my chin to the sun.

I open my eyes. I must move on. Across the other side of the field, more woods and the hill I hope means the gorge and waterway I saw from the ridge. I move forward, passing through the bony green stalks, leaving a laneway of buckled plants in my wake.

I reenter the forested land and once again am besieged by gloom. I scan for water as I go. Sometimes I think I can hear raging rivers, only to step into total silence a few seconds later. The wilderness plays tricks on you like that, like an auditory mirage. Or maybe it's just me.

Occasionally, I encounter dribbling ditches and stop and take some into my mouth. But it never feels enough. I worry about disease, especially with the hovering mosquitoes, which most likely means waterborne larvae. And who knows what other organisms and bacteria may be lurking there?

It's maddening, also, that these little fingers of water never lead anywhere. Downhill or uphill, they just disappear into nothing. There are swimming holes and rivers out here for sure. But they remain hidden in the valleys, or blocked by the walls of green. There's nothing I can do except play the numbers game and hope one of these creeks eventually leads me to a river, then people, then home.

Early afternoon I round a corner of moss-covered rock and smell the fruit before I see it. Plums. Hundreds of the ruby-skinned orbs lie in the grass, bird-pecked and fermenting. I glance up at the tree. A few less-damaged ones cling to the upper branches but it's too far up to climb. So I take my chances on the windblown spoils and crouch down to select the largest plum I can find, wiping away the bugs to take a bite. It's good. Sweet.

I eat more, snatching them up, not caring about the syrup seeping through my fingers and forking at my chin. When I've devoured as many as I can, I sit back on my heels and lick my sticky hands. I feel better, appeased, and wonder if I should try to eat more, but decide the important thing is to continue on because I need to make the most of what is left of the light. Loading as much fruit as I can carry in the skirt of my dress, I set off.

I walk all through the afternoon. It's slow going. A profound tiredness seems to have colonized every part of my body and I struggle not to stumble on my feet. I tell myself that I must keep going, that if I don't find that waterway I will never get out of here.

But less than an hour later, I stop. I look around. No sign of the valley and I'm in dense woods again. A wrong turn somewhere back. Not good.

I blink heavily at my feet and make the decision to nap. Just a short one, I tell myself, then I'll circle back and see if I can find a hill to get my bearings again.

To my left there's a cluster of shrubs and I kneel beneath them, rolling the plums from my skirt and corralling them into a pile. Reaching for drifts of pine needles, browned and brittle from the summer, I rake them toward me, and once buried insects disperse in a frenzy.

When I have enough coverage, I smooth down the points until they all run the same way, and lie on my side, settling my head in the nook of my arm.

My eyelids droop and I feel myself slip. Something skulks on the edge of my mind. A thought I can't quite place. An image I can't really see. Like a song heard only once and not fully remembered.

Whatever it is retreats into the shadows, and I trip my way into a dark and dreamless sleep.

20

I wake up when something crawls over my shin. I leap to my feet. A spider the size of a man's hand is stuck there, an inch below my knee. I give my leg three hard shakes and the thing somersaults and lands upside down on my foot then scutters away beneath a bunch of leaves. I know these things—they build tunnels underground with trapdoors. I think of them all there, lying in wait, beneath the place where I slept.

I dash away before it comes back, glancing around at the failing light in despair. How could I have been so damn stupid to sleep so long? Valuable daylight hours have been lost.

I hurry over the undulating terrain, following the rise and fall of the hills, hoping to find one substantial enough to give me a vantage point across the forest before nightfall. But disappointment waits over every knoll. There's just more of the same laborious, rolling territory. I tell myself not to give up, that one more mound could mean the slope of a steep hill or at least a break in the trees.

But by the time it's dark I'm forced to admit I'm wrong, and have to take shelter in the concave of a thick-trunked tree. I sit shivering, watching the white eye of the moon blink at me, and wonder how much longer I can go on like this. The nights are getting colder and all I have is this rag of a dress. It's a miracle I haven't succumbed to hypothermia already. And the lack of food? How long can I walk without any real sustenance? Then I remember the precious plums I so carelessly abandoned back in the spiders' lair, and feel even more useless than before.

I pick at the crust on my throbbing left foot and think of the Uruguay soccer team and their 1972 plane crash into the side of an Andes mountain. I think about how they were completely alone, how everyone thought they were dead, how no one was looking for them, what they did to survive. They made it out, didn't they? After how many failed attempts? I must be my own plane wreck in the Andes survival story. I will get out. I will make it back. I will live to tell.

*

I wake in the half-light with leaves rattling above my head. Rain. Some of it reaches me down here and I lick my arms. The moisture feels good. Fresh. I sit up and cup my hands to catch the drips but that does nothing except make my palms wet.

I need a container. There's moss growing in bushels at the base of the trees so I reach over and slide my thumb under a thick piece and separate it from the bark then place it out in the open rain. Minutes later, I retrieve the sponge and suck. Not much, but something.

Crouching, I collect six more moss chunks and begin laying them out. I'm going to be in wet clothes with wet hair but at least I'll be hydrated. I wonder if this is the way it's going to be from now on, lurching from one survival crisis to the next, if it's always going to be a double-edged sword. You can have water but it means getting hypothermia. You can have food but it means eating deadwood and insects.

There's a sudden noise. Movement to my left. A pair of eyes flash. My heart leaps. He's back. Rex is back. I open my mouth to scream then stop when I see the rabbit.

Its pelt is dripping and soiled. The pathetic creature blinks at me in disinterest. I realize I'm drooling. I'm disgusted because I want nothing more than to kill the rabbit and suck the flesh from its tiny bones. Could I really do it? Kill a living thing? Eat it raw?

My stomach moans. I lean forward, lift my hand over the rabbit's head, bring it down hard. Miss. The rabbit flees. It's fast, but so am I. In fact, I can hardly believe how fast I can run, that I had this energy in me at all. But I know it won't last, that my legs will soon buckle, that the adrenaline will soon go.

I close in. Ahead the rabbit leaps over roots and rocks. Less than a stride now and I will be able to bring my foot down on top of its head. But the rabbit veers left and I lose sight of it.

I round the corner and see a small cave.

My heart does a little leap. The rabbit is trapped. Soon I will eat.

Moving forward, I stop dead in my tracks. Out of the mouth of the cave steps a dirty gray wolf. The wilting rabbit jolts between the wolf's jaws.

I duck behind a boulder and pray the wolf hasn't seen me. The animal is large, the barrel of its chest broad. A thick black stripe runs the length of its spine to the tip of its tail. He lifts his nose to the wind then drops the rabbit to the ground like a sack. Another wolf emerges to stand beside the alpha, then four more of various sizes, wide-circling the meal in the dirt.

Then the alpha begins. The others join him. There's the sound of cracking bones.

21

A strange thing happens. I feel alive. Acutely alive. My mind is on one thing only. Food and the fact it's highly likely there will be some back there in the den. I forget the pain and the soreness, the discomfort and the cold. I think only of the possible food and how I can get it. The wolves might be more physically powerful than me, especially in a pack, but I can outthink them. I am the one with the human brain.

For an entire day I watch them, careful to keep myself downwind. I arm myself with rocks should they come after me. But they never notice I'm there.

They have no set routine and stick close to the cave. The alpha takes prime spot on top of a flat rock to bask in the weak autumn sun. The others rest under trees or occasionally roughhouse in the dirt. In total, I count seven wolves, including a mother with two rubber-limbed teenagers, whom she is forever kicking away from her drooping teats. There's also an outcast of sorts, a male with a withered hind leg, who skips around the fringes of the pack in a curious lopsided gait.

Twice the pack goes out to hunt. Twice they return with nothing. Then late in the afternoon on the second day, one of the smaller wolves drags a mauled carcass of a bighorn sheep back into camp. The others gather, and I watch from a distance, salivating, as they tear into the meat.

When I come back the next day, the sheep remains are gone, most probably dragged into the den for safekeeping. I sit there in the bushes wondering what to do. I lift my hand. It's as bony as a bat's wing. This is my third day without food. The plums are a distant memory, and the little water I've managed to harvest will not keep me going much longer. I need to carry on south as I had planned. That sheep meat would give me the strength I need to make the journey. I just have to work out how to get it.

The next day my luck turns. Just before sunrise I hear howls. I rush from my shelter to the den. When I get there, the wolves are all gone. I'm not sure why—whether some prey has been spotted or another pack is threatening their territory. Whatever the reason, I need to hurry because there's no telling when they'll be back.

In the dim light, I cross the camp and reach the entrance of the den, pausing there to check over my shoulder. I crouch down and go inside. The first thing to hit me is the odor. Pungent, fatty, like meat left too long, mixed with a ripe canine scent. I wait for my watering eyes to adjust to the dark. But with the sun yet to rise, it's difficult to see anything. From what I can tell, the den is more dugout than cave, with the wolves burrowing further back into the side of the hill.

Unable to stand, I duck-walk a few steps and find myself in total blackness and am forced to poke blindly at things with my fingers. I touch a pile of something, grab two handfuls and pull them out into the emerging daylight. Sticks and bones, old, all shapes and sizes, with the odd patch of fur that could belong to a rabbit, rat, or raccoon. But no meat.

On my knees, I venture in further than before, patting the cool dirt ground as I go. The space gets tight and my shoulders brush against the curved, hard earth. Reaching, I feel out the little wall coves the wolves have excavated.

The smell of meat becomes overwhelming. I'm close. But abruptly I come up against the end of the den and can't go any further. I pause. It has to be here somewhere—the odor is just too strong. My hand hovers across the ground, fully expecting to knock into the carcass, but I can't find anything. I feel out the back wall, thinking maybe I missed a cove. That's when I lose my arm in a hole. A tunnel really.

I look over my shoulder. By now a bulb of light glows at the entrance. If they find me in here I'm as good as dead.

I face the tunnel. It's pitch black and tiny and I won't be able to turn around but what choice do I have? I need food.

I lie down on my front and snake through the opening on my belly. My arms extended out front, I reach into the darkness. Something runs over my spine and I bang my head on the ceiling. I should turn back. Get the hell out of here. Find some berries. Take my chances in the woods.

But I'm close, I know it, so I shimmy in further. The burrow gets tight and I have to squeeze through, angling my shoulders just right, my hips scraping against the hard dirt walls.

I hear something. Oh God, a bark. Distant, but a bark nonetheless. I have to hurry.

I reach out one final time and my hand lands on something sticky. I stretch for it. My little finger hooks around an arch of bone. I sniff my fingertips. Put some to my lips. Grease. Blood. Meat.

More barks. Closer this time. I've got to get out of here. Grabbing the rack of meat, I flatten myself against the ground and move backward. But I'm stuck. I turn my shoulders. It makes no difference, I'm wedged in tight.

Outside the barking gets louder. My heart races. *Hurry. For God's sake, hurry.* I twist my body but the tunnel seems to shrink and it's so black and I'm getting dizzy and I think of the dirt grave and the wolves and the sound of breaking bones. They are going to find me. They will tear my flesh like cloth.

I tell myself I've got to calm down or I'm going to pass out. I tug and tug and finally my shoulders come free. Snaking backward, dragging the meat across the ground, I emerge from the burrow and continue the rest of the way on my knees. Finally I'm close to the entrance, and there's enough room to move up to a crouch.

I turn around.

There's the alpha, hackles raised, looking at me. Close behind, the teenagers nod and squeal. They look at the meat in my hands. I edge forward. The alpha snarls, his gums as pink as a radish. To my left there's a barren leg bone I pulled from the den earlier. I grab it and hold it out.

"Easy."

The sound of my voice stills them but then they start to bark and growl much louder than before. They come closer. I throw the bone at them, then stones, a fistful of dirt.

"Get away!"

All I have left is the meat, so I throw that too. It lands by the mother wolf. The others turn to sniff it, leaving enough space for me to get out and run.

I thrash through the bush and it's not long before they are on my heels. Apart from the loud, steady thump of their footfall, the wolves are silent, no barking or growling, just a focused, determined energy to bring me down.

I round the bend at the rear of the cave and veer left, hoping to see something I can climb. Instead I'm faced with a hill. My chest contracts. I'm blocked in. I turn to face the pack.

A sudden loud clap echoes through the forest. Landslide, I think. Then a second clap rings out and I realize my mistake. Not landslide but gun.

22

The wolves scatter. I spin around, eyes raking the forest. Rex is back. He's back and come to take me away. I look and look, my breath locked in my throat. Try to see him in the shadows. Nothing.

Another shot rings out. I remember, then, how this place plays tricks on you, how sound bounces and skids, makes you believe things are closer than you really think.

What if it's a hunter and not Rex at all? What if it's my big chance to get out of here? I run toward the sound. Pray it's the right direction.

"Hey! I'm lost. Help me!"

Too quickly I'm breathless and forced to bend at the waist and place my hands on my thighs. Then. Voices. Laughter. I cup my hands to my mouth.

"Hey!" I call. "Help!"

I stand listening then hurry forward. Soon I breach the tree line into grassland overlooked by a gray rock mountain. Below the mountain, a river, too wide and fast to cross. On the opposite site of the clearing, there's a Jeep and what looks like an elk tied to the roof rack.

I wave my arm. "Hey!"

The Jeep fires into life. Black smoke jets from the exhaust.

"No! Wait!"

Gears grind and the Jeep rolls forward. I yell and run.

"Stop! Wait!"

But the Jeep just drives away.

I stand there uselessly in the tall grass as the two red eyes disappear into the woods. My legs shake with rage. How could this happen? They were so close. I was so close.

"What do I have to do!" I snatch tufts of brittle grass, throw fistfuls at the woods. "What the fuck do I have to do!"

The grass blows back in my face. But I don't care. I pull out more, tugging stems with both hands, ripping grass from its lodgings, hurling it into the wind. I'm out of control, tearing and pulling, throwing anything I can get my hands on, rocks, stones, pinecones.

I stop and look down at my palms. Both are streaked with blood. I lift my head and blink at the pines. This place. I don't know who I am anymore.

I drop to my knees. I stay there for the longest time. Overhead a hawk wheels. I watch it with my watering eyes.

*

Maybe they'll come back. This is what I'm thinking as I sit in their former campsite tipping the remnants of canned beef stew into my mouth. I use my finger to peel around the inside for gravy then place the empty can on the side with the others. Four in total. Beans and mini franks. Spaghetti-Os. Another beef stew. Lima bean casserole. All of them mostly empty, apart from scraps, congealed and clinging to the bottom and sides. There are other things, too. A blue tarp, sticky with animal blood, three plastic bags, a purple Bic lighter, two sticks of beef jerky, two empty soda bottles, and beer. Three cans of Budweiser. Two full, one three quarters empty. And, of course, nearby is the pounding river, with all that fresh water. In the morning I'll find a safe place to climb down and retrieve some, maybe even bathe. But for now I drink the beer and watch the fire I built from the smoldering ashes the hunters left behind.

The flames are high and phoenix bright. I feel safer, despite the fact I'm more visible. The fire will keep the wolves away, other animals, too. And I'll be warm for the night, at least.

There's no doubt the season is changing. I had deliberately chosen late summer to travel because the trip advice suggested that although the coast would be lit with sunshine all day long, it would be slightly cooler at night. But that advice was meant for further south. I'm somewhere north, maybe even close to the Canadian border.

It's not all bad, I tell myself. I'm not as deep in the wilderness as I thought, and it's only a matter of time before I run into people again. With food, fire, and some meager supplies, I'm better off than I was yesterday.

There's still the problem of my foot, though. I examine the nasty yellow bubble on the underside and wonder what I should do. Leave it or lance it? I decide the latter is best.

Stretching for the empty tin of stew, I peel off the lid, and pass a flame over the sharp edge for a full minute. Then I brace myself and run the tin wheel across the surface of the blister and slice. Out comes the curd. The relief is instant, but the smell sickening. Coaxing the pus a little at a time, I let it drain until there's nothing but a hollow flap of paper-thin skin. I realize then I should have waited until morning, when I had access to the river to rinse the wound properly. I make do with a splash of beer, wincing at the sting.

I feed the fire then lie down, angling my foot close to the warmth, hoping it will dry out some in the night. Now that I've got an open wound I will need to be careful, especially with insects.

23

The next day I wake and inspect my foot. It looks better. A crust has formed and the inflammation subsided. I know I should rest it for a couple of days but I don't have that luxury, I've got to move on. The hunters have not returned in the night and I can't be sure they ever will.

I survey my surroundings. As far as I can tell, there are three options. Scale the mountain. Follow the river. Walk the Jeep's path.

Climbing the mountain will take all day and use what little energy reserves I have left. However, the summit would allow me a vantage point to get a fix on my location, and it could be that the grassland and gorge I saw earlier lie close by, just on the other side of the mountain.

The river, though, could be the better option. Conventional wisdom says where there's water there will eventually be people. But I can't be sure which way to go. Left or right? What if it dries up to nothing like the tributaries I followed previously? And the territory skirting the river may become impassable should I hit mountains or cliffs.

I look over at the space between the trees where the Jeep departed. It's a proven way out of here. Not exactly a road, but the beaten-down path will give me something to follow, which I'm sure will eventually lead to an exit and road.

Before I set out, I take the soda bottles, head for the river, and look for a place to climb down. But mostly the bank is steep, with a sheer drop straight into deep, rushing water. I walk on a little and find a spot I think I can try. Here the bank levels out slightly and I can see stones through the water, shallow enough that I'm not going to be swept away. Taking care, I make my way down, half sliding, clasping vegetation. I reach the bottom of the bank safely but there's nowhere flat to stand. It's simply the bank and the fast-moving river. Crouching, I reach out and touch the water. It's so cold it burns and there's no way I can bathe in it.

I wash my face, though, splash some onto my arms and watch my pink skin emerge from the dust and grime. One at a time, I dip in my feet and bend down to clean the wound. Then I drink as much as I can without bursting. It's a risk, I know, and I feel my core temperature drop right away, but I'll soon be walking again.

I rinse the bloody tarp and fill the two soda bottles—one with a lid, the other without—and place the items in one of the plastic bags and return up the bank.

Back at the campsite, I wrap my feet in the plastic bags and eat half a beef jerky stick. Then with the tarp around my shoulders like a cape and the bag of supplies hooked through each arm, I set out along the Jeep's trail.

Every so often, I call out as I walk, hoping if there are other hunters out here they'll hear me. I also don't want to be mistaken for wildlife and fall victim to a stray shot. But the only thing to bounce back at me is my own voice, hollow and lonesome, so after a while I stop calling to save my energy.

The trail, flattened by the Jeep, is wide and looks like it was once something more substantial. I follow the tire tracks through the forest, hopeful that a proper road will eventually appear, and if not that, another camp.

Around midday, I come to a fork. I stand looking at it. Left seems to lead into thicker woods. Right, the trail widens out. I scan for tire marks but there are none. I choose right, but late in the afternoon the pathway gets narrow and overgrown and I realize I've made a mistake.

I decide to turn back.

A noise stops me. An animal galloping and gaining fast. Mountain lion? Bear? I don't stick around to find out and sprint through the trees, the blue tarp cape crackling as I run. Water from the uncapped soda bottle spills over the rim of my cape and leaks all over my back, and suddenly my load feels light and I realize the bag has split open and I'm losing supplies. But there's no time to stop. The animal is gaining fast.

I run into a clearing filled with tall grass, so tall that I miss the rock, and trip and fall on to my face. I rack my mind for everything I know about how to survive an attack, about not fighting back, about using bear spray if you have it and playing dead if you don't. But realistically I'm in no condition for a fight. I'm a meal for the taking. I can do nothing but cover my head and hope the savaging I'm about to get means I pass out quickly.

Seconds pass. A full minute. I look up. Then I see it. The wolf with the withered leg.

"Son of a bitch."

He stares at me.

"Go on, get!"

I clamber to my feet and stand there looking. He bares his teeth. I shout loudly, and he opens his mouth and issues three clipped barks. Slowly, I bend and pick up a stone and hurl it, nearly connecting with his side. This seems to scare him some and he turns and shuffles through the grass with his tortured lopsided gait then stops a few yards away to stare at me.

If there's one, are there others? I spin around, straining to hear. But there does not appear to be anymore.

I look at the wolf and he looks at me. I can't be sure he's not a threat. Even with his disability, he could still outrun me. But light is falling. I need to carry on. Trying to keep sudden movements to a minimum, I gather what things I can salvage. The uncapped soda bottle has lost all of its water but the other one is still intact. I hunt for the beef jerky but can't find it, and the cans with the scraps are now good for nothing because they are stuck with dust and other debris.

Mercifully, I do find the lighter, hidden in a patch of clover, and while the torn plastic bag is useless for carrying anything, I wrap it around the lighter and tie it to my wrist.

I retrace my steps across the clearing. Behind me the grass swishes as the wolf follows at a distance. I stop and glance around, disorientated. Unable to locate where I was before I took off running, I take a stab and go left. Looking over my shoulder, I see the wolf's head bob through the grass. I feel pity for him and his tiny palsied leg, and think how hard it must be for him to do normal wolf things like hunt.

All through the day, we trudge on. There's no sign of the fork in the road again. For all I know I could be walking in circles. Before long, I'm heading downward into some sort of valley and I wonder if it's the same place I was a few days ago and grow even more disheartened. But when

I round a thicket of gorse, I see, right in front of me, houses.

24

Shacks more than houses. Five of the ancient windowless, rough-sawn shacks sit on flat land no more than half the length of a football field. Nearby there's a crumbling chapel, its fishbone ribs exposed to the elements, a large barn, and a small single-story building with a hitching post out front.

It's clear no one has lived here for decades, if not a century. Lime-green moss blooms across the low-lying parts of the wooden structures, which are blackened and crumbling with age. The space in between is thick and tangled with undergrowth as nature tries to reclaim her land.

The wolf passes me and heads for the waterwheel, which sits motionless in a dry pit that was probably once a reservoir. I approach one of the shacks and push open the door. Single room with a fireplace. Two shelves in the kitchen area. Empty glass jars litter the wooden floorboards. A sapling grows out of a hole in the wall.

I look through the other dwellings. They are almost identical, apart from the odd idiosyncrasy like a badly sloping floor or too low ceiling pitch. Nothing of much use inside. A straw broom. More empty jars. Horseshoes. A wilting, leather-bound Bible.

I cross the street and enter the small building with the hitching post. The walls are lined with empty shelves, and on a wooden desk near the entrance there's an abacus with mahogany beads, and next to that, a ledger. I open it. Neat looping penmanship is blurred and stained with mold.

I go next door to the barn. The first thing I notice hanging from the beams is a pulley system with rusty chains and three giant steel hooks. On the floor, half-hidden in weeds, there's a long double-handled saw, a workbench flipped on its head, a steel pan, and what could be a small pedal-powered band saw.

The entire left side of the barn is gone, which means it's possible to see right through to the chapel next door where the wolf is snuffling through the leaves.

I step through the barn wall into the chapel. Sagging floorboards groan underfoot. The wolf looks over his shoulder at me, his jaw working back and forth, then returns to foraging. Bird droppings are everywhere, calcified on the floor, stuck in hardened drips down the walls. There are nests in the rafters.

The wolf finishes whatever he's doing and disappears outside, and I approach the corner where he was. Among the leaves are scraps of blue eggshells still moist with yolk. Saliva pools in my mouth. *Real food. Protein.*

Pulling a pew close, I step up and reach into a nest and find three small eggs. I fight the urge to crack them open and suck out their contents. Instead I fold them up in the corner of the tarp, and leave through the front entrance where the door is off its hinges. I circle around the chapel in case I've missed anything else. But that seems to be the sum of it.

Light is falling. I need to collect firewood before it gets too dark. In the bramble-ridden area surrounding the buildings, I find a good stock of fallen branches and pinecones, and spy a large lump of sawn timber half hidden in the weeds. I reach to grab it then pull back when I see the tiny white flower. Deadly nightshade. But when I look again, I am thinking the tiny bloom could belong to a potato vine. I probe the earth gently. The ground is soft and moist and comes away easily in my hands. I don't have to dig far to find eight misshapen red-skinned potatoes.

It's too risky to set the fire near the wooden buildings, so I form a small circle of stones in the reservoir pit and fill the ring with wood and light it. I smash a glass jar, take a thick shard, cut up a potato, put the chunks in a steel pan, and place the pan on the fire. When it looks done, I shimmy the pan out with a metal rod I found in the work barn, and break one egg over the top, which cooks almost immediately.

The wolf sits in the leaves on the bank watching. For a moment I worry he might attack me for the food. But he just stares, unmoved, as I spoon the cooked potato and egg into my mouth. And, oh God, it's good. Five Michelin stars as far as I'm concerned. I remind myself to chew slowly. It's been a long time since I've had cooked food and I don't know how my system will react.

When I'm done, I'm tempted to cook more but I don't. Instead I wrap the remaining potatoes and eggs in the torn plastic bag and return to the supply store and place them on the highest shelf to keep them safe from the wolf and other predators.

I settle down for the night, deciding against taking shelter in one of the shacks because I'll be warmer by the fire. I shake out the tarp, wrap it around my shoulders, and throw a bunch of wood on the fire. The wolf looks at me then lowers his head on his paws.

*

I wake in the night to feed the fire. On the bank the wolf has not moved. He is curled up like a bun, the bush of his tail covering his snout. I'm almost jealous of the simplicity of an animal at one with his surroundings, doing exactly what he was supposed to do. Sleep. Eat. Poop. I wonder if he knows what it's like to feel fear.

*

We stay for two nights, me and my lopsided companion. He keeps at least a ten-yard radius between us at all times, as if there's an instinctive natural born restraining order between human and wild animal both to our benefit. He's a useful guide, too. In addition to the eggs, he locates a bush of wild salmonberries and some other root plant that may have been a variation on a turnip. When he makes these finds, I wait a respectful distance until he's had his fill then move in to take what's left.

He discovers water, too, which is an especially significant find since my soda bottle is nearly empty. The small freshwater pond is located a few yards behind the reservoir pit and seems to be fed by an underground aquifer. It's big enough to float around in, so I do, peeling off my plastic bag shoes, the torn dress, getting in to breaststroke the circumference. I turn on my back and watch the trees rock above me.

It's in this dreamlike state, drifting weightlessly, that the thing comes back. The pest of a thing that skirted my consciousness a few nights ago. I close my eyes and try to coax it out into daylight.

My eyes flip open.

Sweet Jesus, I have missed my period.

25

It's a terrifying thought. I do the math, click off the days on my fingers. How long since the gas station? How long since the car? How long since the act? I try and count the nights, starting with now, working backward to the grave, then back from there. All I know is I was annoyed because my period was due to arrive only one day into the trek and I had to make sure I brought enough supplies. I've been out here for way longer than that so there's no mistaking it—I'm more than a week overdue.

So what if I am? It could be the trauma, the punishment meted out to my body, the stress of it all. Being late does not necessarily mean the worst-case scenario.

But even as I think this, I am flooded with doubt. I press my abdomen with my fingers. Could my rapist's child really be growing inside me?

Then another disturbing thought registers—Disease. Herpes. Gonorrhea. *AIDS*.

Oh God, I've got to get out of here. I need to get help, now more than ever. Even though it's late afternoon, I decide to go right now. I gather my supplies, bundle them up in a partially decomposed grain sack, and hurry to the other side of the valley.

The wolf stands and looks at me. For a moment, I don't think he will come but by the time I reach the cypress tree, he's trailing me through the brambles.

As I walk I think of all the other near misses—my friends', my own. Twice before with me. The last time with Matthew at my side, our eyes glued to the wand, waiting for the blue lines that would tell us yes or no. I was almost disappointed when the test was negative. "Next time," Matthew had said, unable to hide his relief, "when we're ready."

Then there was Macy Jones, a girl from junior high I did not know very well, who I found crying in the bathroom after Thursday English class. She told me that no one in her devout Jehovah's Witness family could know, and asked if I would come with her to the clinic. Can't you adopt it out? I said. She shook her head and wouldn't tell me why. It was only later, as we sat in the clinic waiting room, that she whispered that her uncle had been abusing her for over a year.

What if it was too late for me? What if I couldn't bring myself to go through with an abortion? How would I be able to look at the child without seeing Rex's face? And what about the child? How would he or she feel knowing they were a product of rape?

My foot is hurting again so I stop to sit on a flat rock and examine it. My plastic bag shoes have worn through and the wound that was healing so well is now ugly and inflamed. Using a little water to wash it, I fold the plastic bag into a strip and tie it around the bridge of my foot.

I get up and keep moving, pausing briefly to add to my food supplies when I see a handful of black-lipped mushrooms, blossoming along the base of a tree.

By mid-afternoon I top out on a ridge. I look at the rolling hills and valleys, and can find no sign of farmland or the gorge or anything else that signals human life. The sky is mule gray but I can just make out the sun behind the glue. It's to my left, so left must be north, south right.

For another hour at least, we continue south along the ridge until it grows too stony and narrow to progress any further. I circle back down into a gully, the wolf following at a distance, and we walk on until the failing light forces us to stop.

Finding a half-circle of spruce for shelter, I gather wood and undo the burlap bundle to retrieve the lighter. In an instant I see the smashed eggs. I stare at the goo. How could I have been so stupid not to have packaged them better? I pluck out the cracked shells and throw them away and tell myself at least I have potatoes, berries, and a fistful of mushrooms.

I return to the package to hunt for the lighter. But it's elusive. So one by one, I remove each item, lay them all out, pat the ground around me in case I've dropped it. I sit back on my heels and stare at the collection in the half-light. Wherever the lighter is, it's not here with me.

26

I am sick in the night. It comes in waves. Bile spills from my lips, into the dirt, in strange syrupy puddles. The wolf sits watching me, ears pricking every time I retch. It could be the mushrooms or the water or a foot infection. Whatever the source, it's bad.

My sides contract in a fierce spasm and I retch again. I lift my head, gasping, and look through the trees at the corpse-gray sky. I wonder if this is it. I wonder if I have come to the end of the road.

The wolf whines. Then rain is upon us in sudden watery sheets. I do my best to protect myself with the tarp but the rain comes at me sideways. I hate the feeling, the acute ickiness of wet hair sticking to the back of my neck, the thin cotton dress clinging to my skin.

The wolf stands and blinks at me, face dripping. When I don't move, he drops beneath the cedar opposite and rests his head on his paws.

I throw up again and it rains and rains. Heavy, thoroughly, limitless. I think maybe it's a sign. The forest is stronger than I will ever be. Give up. There's no way out. Dying in the hollow of a tree is the best you're going to get. I shut my eyes and try to remember my mother's poor excuse for a Monet above the toilet, and the wrong shade of violet she used for the agapanthus. Then I try to remember her face.

*

The rain continues all through the night and into the next day. The vomiting subsides but I shudder between

102

hot and cold. A fever, which mostly likely means infection. With food poisoning at least there was a chance of the illness passing, but without antibiotics an infection will only get worse.

Finally, I decide to move. I force myself to my feet and take three deep breaths and limp toward to the ridge. The wolf hangs back. It's not until I'm at the stand of redwoods that he follows.

Clutching my meager supplies to my chest, I hobble through the rain, not sure where I'm going. I just listen to the voice in my head. Keep moving. Just keep moving.

As we walk I tell the wolf my darkest secrets. I tell him about the time when I was nine and made three crank calls on a dare at Laura Jane Bettison's slumber party. I tell him about how I stole a pack of colored felt-tipped pens from the bookstore just because the clerk's back was turned. I tell him about how envious I was of all my friends' perfect nuclear families, with Mom and Dad and kids around the dinner table eating supper and thinking nothing of it. I tell him about the summer when I was sixteen and invited to stay with my best friend, Chloe Jenkins, and her family at their beach house in Onondaga **County**, and how I came on to Chloe's father when Chloe and her mother went into town for supplies. He and I were by the pool, side-by-side on the deck, him reading Wilbur Smith, me *Bridget Jones's Diary*. I let my bikini top slip a fraction. At first he pretended not to notice, so I let it fall even further, and he put his book down and said, "What are you up to, missy?" but he was smiling and I smiled back and he leaned over and rubbed his palm over my nipple. But when he realized what he'd done he abruptly withdrew his hand and stammered an apology and got up and left. For the next two weeks I looked at that unfinished Wilbur Smith perched in a mini tent on the side table and thought about what I'd done.

"Maybe that's why I'm here," I tell the wolf. "Maybe I deserve this."

I squint through the rain. There are more important things I should be remembering. The ten things. Kermit. Rex. Numbers on a license plate. But I don't know what else. Oh God, a baby. Not a baby. Please not a baby.

My bad foot gives way and I fall to the ground.

I cry. Everything hurts.

27

I wake up on my front, cheek pressed into the mud. I turn my head and see the wolf figure-eighting back and forth. The rain has cleared but left behind a merciless chill.

Something registers. Through the brush, in the distance, a color. Out of place. It doesn't belong in the wilderness. Orange. Man-made. *A tent.*

Without thinking, I scramble to my feet.

"Hey!"

My leg buckles and I collapse. I get back up again, do my best to ignore the pain.

"Hey! Anyone there!"

I drag my leg behind me.

"I'm sick, I need help!"

I hurry through the trees to the camp and scan for signs of life. The tent is half-collapsed, the left side sagging in on itself, buried in pine needles. Disappointment washes over me. No one has been here for years.

I approach the tent and open the flap. Inside there's a sleeping bag rolled out. A pillow. A Walkman with a cassette. Prince and the Revolution. A flashlight, its rusty batteries oozing manganese oxide. I crawl further inside and look through a small backpack in the corner. Winter clothes, woolen socks, thermal underwear, gloves. I remove my wet dress and put on the foreign clothes, ignoring the spicy scent of a male and mold.

There's a bag filled with six packets of freeze-dried food without use-by dates. I tear one open. But the contents are no more than congealed paste and it's too risky to eat them.

I return to the backpack and find a journal, a wallet, a set of keys. I look at the driver's license. A red-haired guy in the big lips Rolling Stone T-shirt. Born in seventy-two. Alain Dufort.

I open the journal. Its pages mildewed and cracker stiff. Entries fill almost every page in exquisite neat penmanship. All in French. Wedged in the center pages of the journal are photographs—five. A family of four. Mom, dad, son, and daughter at an airport, suitcases at their heels. A man and a woman holding hands. A greyhound nudging a tennis ball in a park. Alain Dufort at a Bruce Springsteen Live in Ramrod concert T-shirt doing the peace sign to the camera.

I flick to the last journal entry, where he had written, in precise English letters—*Snake! 28 November 1989.*

*

I decide to stay and rest. A day at the most. I shake off the leaves and resurrect the tent and get inside.

My foot is in a sorry state. The wet has not helped, and when I examine my sole, it's the color of an avocado left to go bad. I think of trench foot and the open fungal sores soldiers used to get, and how they needed amputations, and sometimes died because their bodies could not take the rot. I can do nothing but wash the lesion with water then bind it with a torn strip of Alain Dufort's underwear, and hope that by some miracle I will make it out soon.

Next, I do an inventory of my supplies. Six potatoes. Two turnips. A quarter-full jar of mushy salmon berries. Eight long-stalked mushrooms I won't be eating again.

Even though I have no appetite, I select a small potato and force myself to eat. It sticks between my teeth like straw.

Afterward, I lift the opening of the sleeping bag to check for critters then crawl inside. Closing my eyes, I feel myself drift. In the bottom left-hand corner my big toe nudges a forgotten balled up sock.

*

I am a child again. The sleeves on my sweater are retreating up my wrists. My mother tells me I must stop growing. My father's study is quiet. I know I shouldn't be in here but I have come for the Golden Gate, to trace its girders, stroke its suspension cables, smell its lubricant on my fingers.

I glance at the turned back of my father. He's bent over his drawing board. A ribbon of smoke curls up from a ginger glass ashtray. I want to stop growing, too. I want to stay here forever, in the dimness of this study, watch my father work, touch the bridge, blink at the halo of lamplight on the ceiling.

My mother calls me. I withdraw to a corner and pull my knees to my chest.

"What are you drawing?" I ask.

He doesn't answer.

"*Show me.*"

Without turning, he says, "You're not supposed to be here."

But he holds up the drawing. A baby without a face, just an opening for the mouth, shaped like an o. I look down at my growing belly, feel it kick. Then he turns around and

I scream. It's not my father at all. It's him, the other man, in my father's chair, holding the faceless baby.

"Take it," he says.

My eyes fly open. I am breathless and ready to run. Orange fabric swells loosely above me. *The tent. I am safe in the tent.* I wipe sweat from my eyes. It doesn't mean anything, I tell myself, it's not a premonition, it's not a sign, I don't know for sure that I'm pregnant at all. I pause then, catching a new thought. What if I made certain I wasn't? What if I was brave enough to take a stick or the wire in the frame of that backpack over there and make sure I wasn't?

I feel sick at the thought. It's too much of a risk. I could hemorrhage. My infection could become worse.

I haul my aching body to a sitting position and peel back the sleeping bag damp with my sweat. My mouth is a cotton ball. I need water so I reach for the backpack.

But the backpack's not there. Twisting, I scan all over. It's nowhere to be seen.

Outside, a noise. Rustling. My pulse begins to race. I reach for the only heavy object I've got—the flashlight—and unzip the flap.

A few feet away there's a shadow and it takes a second to register. A wolf, my wolf, nose deep in the backpack. I stumble from the tent. Potato and turnip fragments litter the ground.

I look at him. "You lousy, greedy, thoughtless son of a bitch!"

He backs away, chewing.

I toss the useless flashlight at him. "Get the hell out of here!"

He darts into the forest.

I get to my knees and stretch for all I can salvage.

28

I wait all night for the wolf to return. I'm sorry I yelled at him. He was doing only what he is programmed to do. Even if it meant stealing from me. At daybreak I shuffle to the edge of the camp and call for him. But there's no sign of him anywhere and after an hour I give up and return to my shelter.

*

In the afternoon, I rouse myself from a thick sleep and hobble outside to a nearby culvert and squat in the leaves. When I'm done, I limp back toward the tent and stumble and fall right on top of Alain Dufort's head. At least that's what I think it is. I stare at what could be a skull and a column of vertebrae. There are fragments of a T-shirt and a pair of pants, too. Using a stick, I lift away the clothes to reveal what's left of Alain Dufort. Nothing more than a collection of bones, most of which are missing, including his arms and legs. But the butterfly of his pelvis is still there tangled in a nest of gama grass, as well as the slender bone of a finger.

Poor Alain Dufort. I wonder what befell him. The snake referred to in the journal? I think of his family who has suffered all these years not knowing where he is.

Close by is a pair of trekking boots still in good shape. I pick them up and shake out three tiny metatarsals. Would it be so wrong? I can hear my mother warning me of superstitions about walking in a dead man's shoes. I try them on. A tight fit but better than nothing. I feel a surge of hope. Tomorrow I will wear these boots and walk myself right out of here.

*

A few hours before dark, the wolf returns. I am hot from the fever and taking in air through the tent flap when I see him. He circles the camp three times then drops into a patch of tall grass. I'm pleased he's back. I watch him sleep. I long to touch the velour of his muzzle, feel his cool, damp nose against my palm. We are kindred spirits, with our various disabilities.

*

I wake before daybreak and lie listening to the wolf run in his sleep. A bashing fist of a headache lobs at the base of my skull. I look at the boots and push them away.

29

A thorough leaden fatigue has conquered my muscles and joints. The tiniest act is an effort. I know I should move on, that I must find food, that I need to get help, but all I can do is lie here in Alain Dufort's sleeping bag and stare at the billowing ceiling.

Outside it's raining. I listen to the patter and think of my little brother and older sister, and wonder what they are doing now. I think of how we once played a game of Monopoly that lasted an entire Labor Day weekend. I think of my mother's basement and the steamer trunk filled with my childhood things, the Barbie dolls I didn't really like, the drug store crossword magazines I devoured, the dress-up clothes three sizes too big. The collection of who I was meant to be. I wish I could go back and open the chest and see what else was inside.

I turn over, run my finger along the seam where the condensation has collected, lick. I have a feeling today is my birthday. September twenty-fourth. If I'm right, I am now thirty-two. Last year my mother had come down from Ithaca and met Matthew for the first time. We went to a Chinese restaurant and ate Szechuan chicken, and pork and chive dumplings. The owner put a candle in a barbeque pork bun and sang Happy Birthday in falsetto.

*

The days and nights bleed into one another and I sleep more and more. I am disappearing. In an effort to preserve its existence my body is consuming itself cell by cell. It emits a strange earthy odor like wild tarragon.

The wolf, too, is suffering. He's barely more than a loose bag of bones. He has taken to sneaking off for hours at a time. I watch him drag himself into the woods, his peculiar, crooked gait more pronounced than ever. I don't know where he goes but he usually returns chewing. Bark, I think. Whatever it is, it's not food because his ribs are protruding worse than mine.

Last night I dreamt I ate him.

Perhaps he dreams of eating me.

I blink at Alain Dufort's things—his boots, his journal, his Walkman—and think how easy it would be to unpick those shoelaces from the eyelets and tie them around my neck. What a blessed release it would be.

I reach up and touch my sunken cheek.

30

A storm bears down in the night and I am shocked awake by flying debris hitting the tent. The tent shakes so violently I'm afraid the fabric will split. I watch helpless as a corner comes loose from its moorings. If I don't secure it, the whole thing will collapse.

Dragging my bad leg behind me, I hurry outside into the howling wind. It's difficult to stay standing as I fight my way through the cold raw hail to the back of the tent. The rear guy line snakes wildly in the air, the metal peg nowhere to be seen. I need a rock or some other heavy object to weigh it down, but before I can find anything, the other rear corner comes loose, then the two front ones. The tent lifts off the ground and levitates before me. It shoots upward, spiraling and spitting out contents then snags high in a tree. I stand watching it. Icy needles rattle my skull.

The wolf is barking and the push and shove of the wind finally gets me moving. I stagger down the hill and turn left and try to keep moving forward. *Shelter. Find shelter.* But in the darkness I'm as good as blind and suddenly I am felled by something I do not see.

*

When I rouse, I feel calm. There's a soft silence. At first, I think I am deaf, that my body is shutting down one sense at a time. But when I open my eyes I see snow float in feathers above me. Everything is shrouded in white, the tops of the pines, the forest floor, the spikes on the thorns, me.

I stay there, not wanting to move. I am dreaming a beautiful dream. Nature has come to take me away.

Then a sound arrives. A gentle sound. It means something, but I don't want to think, all I want is the snow. But the noise takes shape, trickles into the shells of my ears. Trickling? Not trickling, gushing. *Water.*

I lift myself up and stumble toward the sound. Trees thin out. The air feels full, fresh, wet. I look down. I'm standing on the precipice of an enormous, roaring waterfall. It thrashes into the boulders below. These boulders sit in white rapids that belong to a reptilian monster of a river— deep and treacherous and wide. A mile down the waterway, the bridge and sheer cliffs of the gorge.

I call for the wolf. But he's nowhere to be seen. I call again. A flash of gray zigzags through the trees and the wolf steps from the forest's edge. He pauses there, his paws sunken in the snow.

Turning from him, I limp toward the bridge through the mantle of white. The wolf trails me, the shush of his footfalls behind me a comfort. Halfway I stop to lick stamps of snow from my palm then continue along the bluff. My energy is failing and I'm barely able to remain upright, but I keep going until I reach the gorge.

We stand looking. The bridge is impassable. The first ten feet of planks have rotted away. The next twenty-foot stretch hangs in midair like a ladder.

In the crags and cracks of the sheer gorge cliffs, tendrils of green spill out and host a bright pink flower. A black-winged falcon wheels through the gully.

I turn to thank the wolf, face the cliff, and jump.

Return

31

I fall through the misted air and plunge into the frigid water below. Tossed over and over, I am a tiny leaf, grasping at anything—rocks, branches, the water itself. But I'm too fast-moving. My head goes under and I can't raise it up again and I'm dragged down deep until I'm bouncing like a baby and I try to claw my way back up and my blood is turning to ice and my lungs are filling with silt and then, all at once, the washing machine stops and there's daylight and oxygen and I am sucking in air and coughing out water.

I raise my head. I have been spat out into a tributary and there's an embankment to my left. Paddling forward, I keep going until I feel pebbles underfoot then haul myself on to dry land and collapse on the cold, snowy stones.

My ragged breath ghosts the air as I lift my arm and look at my shattered wrist. I can't feel a thing. But the rest of my body could have been smacked by a truck.

*

I come to on the frozen stones. It's sleeting. I need to move. I squint through the curtain of icy rain and look for a road or some other pathway. To my left I see something. Set back in the woods about fifty yards sits a single-story cabin. Out of its corrugated tin roof juts a chimney chugging smoke.

*

I force myself to my knees then to my feet. My clothes are heavy and wet and dragging me down. Pushing through the pain, I heave myself up the bank and hobble away from the cabin toward the forest. Shielded by the trees, I circle back and crouch behind a bramble bush and pause, shivering, to study the house.

A hip-high stone fence made from chunks of large bronze river stone is dissected by a small wooden gate that opens out onto a pathway leading up to a porch. On the porch in the corner is a lone high-backed rattan chair, with a box for a footrest. By the door, under a clean single window, sits a pair of large brown leather work boots.

I don't open the gate. Instead I approach the rear of the cabin, where two back windows are lit with soft light. I drop back into the shadows. Stacked neatly under the shelter of the eaves is firewood cut in precise single-foot lengths. Nearby, a small generator hums and peppers the air with diesel.

The yard is a decent size, and over the way there's a wire-fenced pen with goats and sheep, and an adjoining pigpen and chicken coup. Next to that is a garden with rows of carrot tops, broccoli, string beans, and beets. A barn, not much bigger than the cabin itself, is located at the end of the yard.

A wave of exhaustion hits me. Inside my drenched clothes, my body shudders and jerks. I lift my eyes to the barn and stumble toward it. Avoiding the front shutter doors, I see a side entrance and go there to peer through the gaps in the wood, but it's too dark to see inside. I lift the latch, push open the door, and stand there listening.

I inch forward, close the door behind me, and wait for my eyes to adjust to the dark. The barn looks smaller from the inside and is filled with all manner of things. But everything is orderly and in its place. Above a work bench, tools hang from nails on the wall. In the vise an axe waits to be sharpened. On the side opposite there are sacks of animal feed, and garden equipment including a shovel, hoe, and rake. A rough-sawn staircase leads to a loft.

In the middle of the barn, taking up most of the space, a vehicle hides beneath a khaki-colored cover. I approach it and let my hand linger on the roof. I picture the mint Capri, Kermit the Frog, the trunk with all of the things.

I throw back the cover. A black VW Beetle, front tires flat, rear ones on blocks. The hood is missing, the engine long gone. I let out a breath and circle the vehicle and release the axe from the vise, then limp past four barrels labeled *Hawkins Oil Refinery*, and haul my body up the steps to the loft. I lie on my side and face the gaps in the wall, clutching the axe. Dust stirs on a splinter of light.

32

When I wake up there's a shotgun pointed in my face.

"I use it, don't think I won't."

I squint at the elderly, small-boned Asian woman through the fuzz of my vision, shotgun snug on her shoulder.

"You a junkie?" she demands.

"I was kidnapped."

"Bullshit."

"It's the truth, ma'am."

But as soon as I say it, I am wondering to myself, is it? I've been in the wilderness for so long I might have made the whole thing up. What if I got lost? What if I'm delirious? Then I remember about the ten things, the baby.

"From a gas station in Oregon."

The woman finally looks like she might believe me.

"Please," I say, shuddering. "I'm so cold."

She lowers her gun.

"I don't like this," she says, looking over her shoulder. "You make problem for me."

"I won't, please—"

Before I can finish, a coughing fit grips me and I throw up at least three liters of water. The woman reaches down and puts the back of her hand against my forehead and murmurs something I don't understand.

*

I sleep a dreamless, blissful sleep for what seems like an eternity. Warm and sound and soft. Like I'm drifting on a marshmallow. When I open my eyes, I find myself on a lumpy sofa swaddled in a green woolen blanket. Directly opposite, a fire glows in the grate. A large black headless bearskin partially covers the wooden floor, and in the corner, on top of a small table, there's a tiny shrine comprised of a miniature brass Buddha, a clutch of smoking incense sticks, and a burning pillar candle. On the wall above the shrine hangs a framed photograph of a white man in military uniform.

"You been in forest long time?" It's the Asian woman. She's at the beige Formica table playing a game of solitaire. She glances at me when I don't answer. "Cat eat your tongue?"

"Where am I? Which state?" I ask.

She lifts the old-fashioned tortoiseshell pipe to her lips and puffs. I can smell the harsh tobacco from here.

"Washington."

The woman knocks the ash from the pipe into a saucer and gets to her feet. She takes two steps into the adjacent kitchen area and opens a cupboard to retrieve a plate.

"Must eat. Nothing left of you."

She reaches inside an old-fashioned pull-handled fridge to take out what looks like cheese and bread. I sit up and see that my foot has been dressed in a clean white bandage, my broken wrist, too.

"Very bad," says the woman, glancing at my foot. "Will try medicine."

"Medicine?"

She points to her chest. "I make medicine. For foot. Maybe get better, maybe not."

She puts a tray on my lap. On the plate there's a generous hunk of crusty bread and a wedge of cheese.

"Homemade. My goat, Betty, she give good milk."

The woman returns to her card game and relights her pipe.

I raise the sandwich to my mouth and chew. Food. Real food. I can't remember how long it's been since I ate anything that resembles a sandwich.

The woman lifts her eyes from her cards. "Slow down or you sick up again."

I do my best to be more measured but end up demolishing the sandwich more quickly than is probably wise.

"What's your name please, ma'am?" I say when I come up for air.

"Nhung."

"Thank you for the food, Nhung, and for looking after me." I pick up the mug of tea on the side table and take a sip. "I'm Amelia Kellaway. What is the date please?"

"Date?"

"Day of the month?"

"Seventeenth."

"Of September?"

"October."

"You're joking." I've been lost in the wilderness for over a month.

I'm overcome with emotion and bury my face in my hands and cry. "I thought I was going to die out there."

"The man who took you, he interfere with you?"

"Yes."

"Son of bitch."

The crying drains me and I'm sleepy again. I lie back down in the nest of blankets and watch the flames bob in the hearth.

"Don't you get lonely out here all by yourself?" But I fall asleep before I can hear the answer.

33

For the next three days snow keeps us inside, apart from when Nhung bundles herself up in a heavy-duty jacket and ventures out to the backyard to empty the ash pan or feed her small menagerie of animals that consists of, as far as I can tell from my vantage point in the kitchen window, two pigs, three goats, four sheep, an unspecified number of chickens, and a deer. Nhung tells me the cabin is powered by a generator, which is powered by gasoline that Nhung keeps in the barn. She doesn't have a working vehicle and because it's a two-day walk to the closest neighbor, someone from the county drops off supplies once every two months.

The next visit is due in five weeks. We both know that's too long to wait. My foot is getting worse despite Nhung's best efforts and her twice daily treatments of applying her pungent concoction, a lumpy brown paste that smells vaguely of spoiled milk. The foot is totally useless and I can't put any weight on it. A grape color has started to climb my calf like a vine.

In the barn there's a dusty long-range two-way radio and Nhung retrieves it and every three hours winds it up to call for assistance. But the radio is old and Nhung tells me it often stops working during big snowfalls and storms and for other unexplained reasons. It belonged to her husband, Jack. The man in the photo. As a sixteen-year-old, she met Jack at a refugee camp in the 1970s when she and her family fled the Khmer Rouge. He was an American military liaison officer.

"Jack worked for the man who own this land—Mr. Hawkins, oil refinery man. He very rich and like Jack a lot. He help build this house and let us stay for as long as we want. That twenty year ago now. Then Jack got sick."

"I'm sorry."

Nhung frowns and smooths more ointment onto my dismal foot.

"The cancer," she says.

She nods toward the window. "He under the ponderosa."

I think about how every night Nhung kneels in front of the tiny shrine, chanting softly, palms pressed together in prayer, the flame of the candle bobbing with her breath.

"You had no children?" I say.

She shakes her head. "Born still."

Wiping the ointment from her hands with a cloth, Nhung lifts her shirt to reveal a zigzag of scars across her lower abdomen, bulbous and red and thickened with time. It looks like she's been hacked at with a blunt piece of tin.

"Two boy, one girl," Nhung says as she slips her shirt back into her pants. "Khmer rape me when I ten. Hurt inside where baby grow."

"I'm so sorry."

She tucks a wisp of gray hair behind her ear. "Sons of bitches will go to hell."

She turns her attention back to my foot and finishes with the ointment then wraps it with a bandage. She looks at me. I know what she's thinking. She mentioned it yesterday when she unfurled the bandage, sodden with my bodily fluids, and threw it into the fire like she'd done with the rest. The two-day walk to the neighbors'.

I grasp her hand. "Don't leave me."

"You need doctor."

I grasp tighter. "*Please.*"

"Okay," she says finally, getting to her feet. "I try radio again."

*

I shudder awake. It's night. The firelight draws an apricot ghost on the ceiling. Nhung is at the window looking out. She glances at me when she sees me awake.

"I get through. Someone be here soon. Take you back. See doctor. Police."

Police. Real life. I don't like the sound of it, perverse as it seems, given what I've been through. Logically I know I can't stay here in the warm, safe bubble of Nhung's home, but nothing about any of this is logical. I fight the urge to tell Nhung that I don't want to go and instead let her help me to her bedroom, the only other room in the cabin.

She points to the old-fashioned pitcher and basin of steaming water. "You wash. Put on fresh clothes."

She leaves me and I glance around at the neat plain walls, the large bookcase stacked with Harlequin romance novels, the crumpled black-and-white photograph wedged beneath the frame of the mirror—her and four siblings and mother and a bespectacled man who must be her father.

I remove the flannel nightgown and dip the cloth in the water and wipe my skin. I turn to look in the mirror. Reflected back is a body I don't recognize, thin and slack and covered with bruises. I run a fingertip over the tracks of my ribs and say a prayer of thanks to my body for carrying me to Nhung.

128

I slip into fresh clothes that smell like lemon soap, and walk over to the bookshelf and select a well-thumbed Harlequin. I tear out the blank back page and pick up the pen from the dresser and write *Thank you* then put the note under Nhung's pillow.

There's a rumble outside. A car engine. I sit down on the end of the bed and take a deep breath. I think of all that's to come—the city they will take me to, the doctors who will inspect and swab, the probing questions of detectives with pens and note pads, the explaining myself over and over. For a moment, I consider opening the window and fleeing back into the woods.

But before I can make good on this insane impulse, I hear the snap of the car door close, followed by a crunch of boots then voices in greeting.

It's time. There's no going back. I get to my feet, smooth down the bedspread, and hobble over and open the door. I blink, confused, at Nhung and the man standing next to her.

"Hello, Amelia," says Rex. "I heard you were having a lick of trouble."

34

I can't move. The air has been sucked from the room. Rex in blue jeans. Plaid flannel shirt. Green puffer jacket with a Hawkins Oil Refinery logo.

I plunge a knuckle in my eye. Open. Blink. He's still there.

"This Mr. Hawkins," says Nhung. "Jack's old boss. He good guy. He look after you now." She stares at me and frowns. "What wrong? You white ghost."

My mouth is cotton. I glance at Nhung, who is looking at Rex like he's the greatest American hero, and I begin to doubt myself. Maybe it's not him. Maybe it could just be the fact he's a man. Maybe my fried brain is making all the wrong connections. I shake my head, literally shake my head, and look again. Then he does that thing, lifts his forefinger to rub the spot just above his top lip, and I know this is no mistake.

"You're bleeding," says Nhung, pointing.

I glance down. Blood is trickling down the inside of my thigh. I look at Rex.

"It's him," I say.

"What you mean?"

Rex turns to Nhung. "I put a gas can out the back for the generator. That should see you through the month."

"He's the one that took me from the parking lot."

"And a sack of feed for the chickens."

"The one who raped me."

Rex looks at Nhung. "It's the shock, Nhung. I take no offense."

Nhung pauses and stares at me. "You confused. Mr. Hawkins our neighbor. Respected community man. He good guy."

I take a step back. "He kidnapped me and took me to the woods and raped me and left me for dead."

Nhung shakes her head, glances at Rex. "Don't say these things."

"It's him. I know it is," I say.

Rex places his hands on Nhung's shoulders and looks at me over the top of her head.

"Trauma can do funny things to a person, Nhung," he says. "Amelia will be better once the doctor sees her. Speaking of which, we should get going before that second snow front moves in."

I take a step back. "I'm not going anywhere with you."

I glance to my right, see the shotgun in the kitchen corner, way out of reach.

"I wouldn't," says Rex, following my eyes.

"Leave us alone." My voice trembles and I hate the way it sounds so weak. "Get in your car. Turn on the ignition, just drive away."

"So you can report me to the police? Oh no, Amelia, jail isn't for me."

Nhung frowns. "What you saying, Mr. Hawkins?"

"What I'm saying, Nhung, is that Amelia here is a problem and so are you."

Nhung pivots to look at Rex, but his hands close around her throat and he tightens his grip.

"Stop it!" I cry.

But he's not listening. His jaw is set, determined, as if he's breaking concrete with a pneumatic drill. Nhung tries to pry his hands away and swings her head back and forth, but it does no good. I lunge for him and jump on his back and gouge his eyes. He cries out and flings me off and I tumble backward and knock my head on the stove. Glass jars fall from the shelf above and shatter on the ground. Momentarily stunned, I need a few seconds to focus. When I look up, a limp Nhung is sliding from his hands onto the floor. Poor sweet, innocent Nhung.

He takes two steps toward me. I stagger to my feet and press myself against the wall.

"Stay away from me."

I glance at the door. Outside is his truck. A chance to get away. I bolt. Rex grabs me, hands locking around my throat. I struggle and kick and try to knee him in the groin but the edges are growing closer and grayer, like I'm too far underwater to get back to the surface. I taste blood, feel the gristle of my tongue between my teeth. I try one last time to elbow him in the gut, but it lands softly, and I hear him laugh and whisper in my ear.

"Always the fighter."

35

I open my eyes. I am in a sitting position, upright against the kitchen wall. Tiny cubes of glass are stabbing my thighs. Something is stuffed in my underwear, a dishcloth.

"You weren't fooling this time, you really did get your monthly."

Rex sits on the floor directly opposite, gun resting on his thigh. Just behind him, Nhung is lying prone and still.

"She's in a better place," he says, not turning around.

There's a bloody half-crescent under his eye from where I gouged him that's beginning to bruise.

"I'm proud of you, Amelia, really proud. You survived out there when most wouldn't have stood a chance. I underestimated you."

I squint at him through the gauze of pain. How can any of this be real? How can Nhung be dead? How can Rex be here?

"Please, I can't take anymore."

"Don't be weak," he says, sharply. "That's not you."

"Why don't you just shoot me?"

He shrugs. "Maybe I want you to stick around for a while." He leans close. "Maybe I'm beginning to respect you."

He takes a breath and runs a hand over his face.

"You know I once saved a car full of kids? Their white trash mother pushed the minivan right into the lake. She was standing on the bank watching it sink when I drove past. When I got out of my truck, I saw three kids slapping the windows and hollering for help, and she was just standing there like it was any other day. I dove in, smashed the glass, pulled them out one by one, even gave the smallest boy mouth-to-mouth until the ambulance got there." He blinks at me. "What kind of mother would do that to her own kin?"

I close my eyes. Everything hurts. Every muscle and joint. Every fiber of my being. The sound of his voice.

"I'm not all bad, Amelia."

I think of the wolf.

"Open your eyes, Amelia."

I think of how close I was to making it home.

"Look at me."

I pry open my lids.

"Tell me about the day he left."

"Who?"

"Your pop."

Did his cruelty know no bounds? Did he have to take everything from me?

"Easy guess, Amelia. You have that little girl lost quality. There's a loneliness in you. I have it, too. I know what it's like when people let you down. It leaves you with a hole that can't be filled."

"I won't talk about that."

"It must have hurt to know he didn't want you. Did you cry yourself to sleep?"

"Please be quiet."

"Did you see his likeness in every suburban mall? Curl up with his favorite shirt? Miss him at the Christmas table?"

"Stop it."

"Amelia, tell me about the pain."

"It nearly destroyed me—is that what you want to hear?"

"Keep going."

"Go to hell," I say.

He smiles. "You and me, we're a lot alike."

"You've got to be joking."

"Most women are as dull as dishwater, but not you, Amelia. Your daddy didn't deserve such a smart and beautiful daughter." He cocks the gun and points. "Tell me more."

"I don't know what else you want me to say."

"Did you ever see him again?"

"When I was thirteen I caught a glimpse of him in a Target store, but by the time I made it to the aisle he was gone. Then I saw him at the intersection in a gray late-model Nissan. I begged my mom to stop but the car had already driven off."

Rex looks sad. "Like I say, he didn't deserve you."

"It's in the past."

He pauses and stares at me. "There's something else."

"No."

"You're holding back. I know you better than you think, Amelia."

"I told you, he left. I never saw him again."

"Did he abuse you?"

"Of course not," I stammer, but I feel something, the black heart of that long ago time rising up from the depths of my soul.

"You're crying," says Rex.

"Am I?"

"Yes."

Oh, and it hurts, this feeling, like I'm right back there again, the day I climbed the stairs to his study.

"And shaking."

"Please," I say. "Please stop."

"Tell me what happened, Amelia."

And I see me, nine years old, carrying the tray with his lunch, leftover pasta bake, a packet of saltine crackers, tumbler of blackcurrant juice, and the little card I made for him that said "Time for lunch" in pink felt-tipped pen. I'm turning left on the landing, taking the stairs one at a time, hearing the cutlery rattle and being careful not to splash the juice over the side of the glass and onto the white paper napkin, and reaching the closed study door and balancing the tray on my knee with one hand and using the other to turn the knob, and pushing open the door and the tray slipping from my hands when I see my father's sock-covered feet swinging right in front of me.

"I found him," I whisper in disbelief. "I thought he must be playing a trick. Then I saw the chair, kicked away, heard the sound of rope rasping against the wooden rafter."

"Oh, Amelia."

I'm sobbing now and I bury my face in my hands and it all becomes clear, those hazy images on the edge of my dreams, my loathing for blackcurrant juice, the scar just below my left knee from running out of the room and tumbling down the stairs and landing on a nail on the second to last step.

Rex lays his hand on my shoulder. I look up and he's frowning.

"You didn't deserve that," he says. "Let me take care of you, Amelia. We'll go away, just the two of us, live a simple life."

Behind him, Nhung moves. At first I think I'm imagining it—that she's still alive—but then Nhung opens her eyes and stretches for the shotgun.

"You know how I got rich, Amelia?" says Rex. "It was my uncle's land. My bitch of a mother sent me to live with him when I was five. A little kid didn't fit with her objectives in life, which were to sleep with every man who paid her even the slightest bit of attention. Uncle Ron worked me like a slave. He beat me and whooped my ass just for fun. I slept on the barn floor with the pigs until I was fifteen years old, until the day I got in that wheat thrasher and drove right over him and tore that bastard limb from limb, the same day the sludge bubbled up from the well at the back of the property and erupted like a god damn geyser. That dumb son of a bitch had been sitting on millions and didn't even know it. By then my mother was dead from God knows what venereal disease so as his only living relative, I got it all." He looks at me. "But I'm prepared to leave it all behind. The money. Everything. I would do that for you."

I steady my breath and wipe my tears and try not to let on to what's happening behind his back.

"You would?" I say.

Nhung picks up the shotgun and nods at me. I look at Rex, pulse racing, thinking this is my and Nhung's only chance, so I push the image of my father's swinging body to the back of my mind and take a deep breath.

I roll onto my side and a shot rings out. Rex yells in pain and looks over his shoulder at Nhung. She fires again, but he ducks, and the shotgun blast gets me. A dozen hot pokers slam into the tenderest parts of my flesh.

Rex is moving now, grabbing a log, charging at Nhung, and smashing it down on top of her head. There's an ungodly crack as she crashes to the floor in a heap. He pivots and we both see his gun on the ground.

I reach it before he does. I lift and point.

"Amelia."

I fire a shot into his chest. Darkness spreads across his gray shirt. He stumbles backward into the tiny shrine, knocking the candle, where it rolls off the table and onto the stack of papers, which bursts into flames.

"Amelia," he wheezes.

Rex staggers in a circle and tries to say my name again but nothing comes out. He drops to his knees then falls forward on his face and lies there as still as a rock.

The gun rattles in my hand. I killed him. The monster is dead.

A window explodes. The fire is raging through the tiny cabin. I have to get out. I fight my way through the dirty black smoke over to Nhung and grab her feet and make it as far as the bearskin rug before giving up. I'm too injured and the fire's too fierce. Above my head a beam is beginning to crack so I leave Nhung's body and lunge for the door and make it outside before I hear the beam collapse behind me.

I reach Rex's truck, lift the radio, press the button, shout.

36

It comes in flashes. The whoosh of the copter blade. The spray of cold as they lift me onto the stretcher. Smoke. The smell of burning bodies. Many hands upon me, tugging and cutting my clothes. Someone is screaming, *What the hell happened down there?* Another voice yells, *She's losing blood, apply pressure before she bleeds out!*

Somebody shakes me. "Ma'am, how many people are in the house?"

I can't breathe.

"*Ma'am.*"

"Two," I wheeze.

"Who shot you, ma-am?"

I try and think of his name but can't remember.

"Truck," I say.

"She says there's a truck down there. Get them to check."

A few seconds later, the pilot shouts over her shoulder, "That's a negative on a vehicle."

I shake my head. "Black truck."

The pilot radios the team on the ground again. "She's adamant there's a truck. Look again."

"Ma'am, who owns the vehicle?" says the paramedic.

"The man who shot me," I gasp.

The pilot cuts in, "There's no truck."

I shake my head. "Not possible."

"Calm down, ma'am."

"Not possible. I killed him."

"Heart rate is elevated."

"Ma'am, you've got to calm down."

"Truck. Truck. Truck."

"She's in distress. Get me some midazolam ASAP."

I feel a dull prick and lava floods my veins. Suddenly I remember his name. Rex Hawkins. And five of the ten things. Kermit the Frog. Aviator sunglasses. Wood-beaded seat cover. Partial plate O, K, and 4. A son called Noah.

I move my lips but no sound comes out. The paramedic comes closer.

"What was that?"

"He's not dead."

Epilogue

I watch Lorna pour water into a tumbler and sit back down in her leather executive chair.

"Will that be in your report?" I ask.

She smiles. "Our sessions are confidential, Amelia. You know that."

"I want this job."

"I understand." She sips the water, sets it down on the glass-topped coffee table between us. "Why do you think my report will be unfavorable? Have you been holding back?"

I think of the eight months of therapy, telling her what she wants to hear. My hand curls around the cane.

"How's the physio going?" she says.

I shrug. "Doing the rumba is pretty tough with half a foot."

"How do you feel about that?"

I look at her. "Really?"

She lifts her hand. "Sorry. Patronizing."

Pivoting, she retrieves a bright blue folder from her desk and opens it.

"It's bound to be high pressure. Being a state prosecutor is not going to be a walk in the park. Especially if you are fragile."

"I'm not fragile."

"You want to help."

"Yes."

"There are other, less stressful, ways to help people, Amelia."

I try to soften my face. "Please, Lorna. I know I can do this. I just need a clean psychological assessment."

Behind her, out the window, pigeons are nesting in the stone gargoyles.

"And him?" says Lorna.

"What about him?"

"It can't be a great feeling knowing he's still out there."

I don't tell her about the hang-up phone calls. The three deadbolts on my front door. The guns stashed in every room of my apartment.

"I'm not going to let Rex Hawkins control my life."

She shoots me a smile. "Good for you, Amelia. But you need to be careful. I'm not just talking about physical safety here, I mean emotional too."

"I know the signs."

She nods. "That's important."

I look at the tiny Dictaphone on the glass coffee table, barely the size of a pack of gum, at the pinprick of red light and the tiny, hollow slit, recording everything I say.

Finally Lorna speaks. "Okay."

"Okay?"

"I'll clear you," she says. "But you need to come in every second week. There's still work to do."

My heart leaps and I feel an unfamiliar boost.

She looks at her watch. "That's time."

Lorna rises and I follow her to the door.

"Go do good in the world, Amelia."

*

I step out onto the pavement, button my parka at my throat, and head left. My cane wobbles beneath the weight of my hand. I'm still not used to this third leg and the fact

I will have to live with a limp for the rest of my life. But it's the cane or a wheelchair.

"Hey, lady, spare a dollar?"

I ignore the shifty guy in the yellow Nikes and carry on, clomping up the street, avoiding missteps in the cracks.

"God bless," he calls anyhow.

You too, I think, God bless you and your sorry state and the cardboard box you crawl into at night with the bottle of whatever you can get your hands on but I don't stop for strangers anymore.

Downtown traffic roars by, tourists take selfies, a guy in a Yankees cap sells dolls from the trunk of his battered Honda. I head south, past Central Park and into the diner on East 45th Street. My mother is talking to the waitress about the best way to steam okra. I go over and she folds me into a hug of turpentine and home-baked bread.

"Hey there, sweets. How you doing?"

I spy the crusts of aqua paint in the crescents of her forefinger and thumb.

"Better than average."

THE END

More books you'll love in the Amelia Kellaway Series...

Coming for You (#2 Amelia Kellaway)
By Deborah Rogers

A brutal crime. A traumatized mind. A victim no one believes...

Amelia Kellaway is hiding a secret. Still deeply traumatized by the kidnapping incident she suffered three years ago, Amelia is struggling to cope with a crippling anxiety disorder where she compulsively checks her locks and doors. She's also experiencing frightening blackouts that strike at random. The root cause of her anxiety is her unshakable belief that her previous attacker, Rex Hawkins, is stalking her. She's been to the authorities but they've dismissed her concerns as the paranoid delusions of a traumatized mind.

But are Amelia's fears really unfounded? Could Rex Hawkins still be out there, waiting for her to drop her guard and make a mistake? Or is Amelia slipping deeper into neurosis and at risk of losing her mind?

Another gripping tale of psychological suspense from Deborah Rogers, *Coming for You* is a terrifying portrayal of a young woman on the brink, with shades of Hitchcock and Gillian Flynn.

EXTRACT

Coming for You

1

I hate this. This half life. This half foot. So I come here to forget. To the subway. To just sit and imagine all of the things. All of the netherworld places beneath my feet. The warrens and laneways and sewers and tunnels and secret entrances and exits. The underground people pulling their underground carts into even more underground places. The rats and snakes and blind feral cats lurking and leaping and scuttling. Along and beneath the hot iron tracks, way down below through the cracks in the walls and the holes in the ground.

I come to ride the trains. Late at night when there are not too many people around. When I can get a fix on who exactly is in the car. When there's enough empty space to escape if I have to.

I get on anywhere and just sit and let the train take me away. I like the slipping and sliding on the blue plastic seat, the push and shove of the stop and start, the jerking and rolling, the thump of the wheels on the track. I like how no one looks at me and I don't have to look at them. I like how I can forget who I am and who I was meant to be and the gaping canyon between the two. I like how I don't have to think about the present, future, or past. Especially the past.

I ride and ride and ride. Sometimes for hours. I ride until the stale air tightens my face and the strange heartbeat of the train quiets my mind. I ride until all the thinking and dark thoughts abate. That's the goal anyway. Because if I'm honest, he never really goes away. My constant unwanted companion, who tumbles around my skull like a lone sneaker in a dryer, the rubber fixing to blister and melt in the heat of the barrel. He never lets go of me and I never let go of him. We are Siamese twins. Bound together by the crimes he committed against me and my soul.

But at least here on the train I can sit and pretend he does not exist. And pretending is better than nothing. Pretending is all I've got and I want to hold on to that for as long as I can.

I know the night's journey will end at some point and that I can't ride the train forever. After a few hours I will have to return to the real world above, where he does exist, and eventually I will, raising myself up from the seat to stand on my one good foot and steady my cane in my hand and clap myself out of the subway car and up the stairs and back into the savage world.

But for now, I am here, thinking and not thinking. For now, I can let myself breathe.

Tonight I count the number of people in the car with me. Three. A gray-haired woman in a fluoro jumpsuit and Birkenstocks sits opposite. A regular guy in blue jeans and a bomber jacket leans against the pole thumbing through his phone. A girl too young to be out this late on her own stands by the door staring into the flying darkness. I can see her face in the reflection and she catches me looking. She casts a sudden bold look at me over her shoulder as if to say what the hell are you looking at? I wonder what she sees in return, this woman with a cane in her sensible navy trouser suit. There goes one hell of a broken human being? A survivor? Am I survivor? Or did I really die back there in the woods?

I glance away and she returns to the window and the dark tunnel walls flip by.

Above me, someone has scratched the words *Pound Town* into the ceiling of the subway car. I imagine a youth in a hoodie teetering on top of the seat, arm hooked through the railing, stretching with a knife to carve those words into the steel. Maybe his friends goaded him on. Or maybe he was a loner like me and simply wanted the world to know he existed. I wonder if he ever returns to admire his work. If he stands amongst the rush hour commuters, quietly triumphant, holding his secret close.

The train pulls into a stop. I glance up, as I always do, checking for who's about to get on, and see them. A sea of expectant faces waiting on the platform. There are so many of them, so many faces, that I cannot possibly catalog each one. My heart pulses in my throat. The doors open and in comes the rush. All those chattering faces push their way in and fill up the car, swallowing up all that nice empty space. A well-to-do crowd in suits and tuxes and sequined dresses. In they come, pushing and laughing, fanning themselves with programs, diamante chandelier earrings swaying and winking. In they come, squeezing in on the seat beside me, standing around and over me, pressing in on all sides.

My throat goes tight. It's not safe. I'm no longer safe. Three has become dozens, all crammed together. They are too close. Everyone is too close. He is here. He is everywhere. I have to get out.

I wake up on the cold hard floor. In front of me, shoes, lots and lots of shoes, all pointing in my direction. Polished black oxfords. Brown leather loafers. Strappy Jimmy Choos. High heels and kitten heels. A pair of battered Birks and an overgrown toenail.

I am flipped on my back. People loom over me.

"You dropped like a stone." A bald, rotund man in a blue sweater crouches next to me then tries to steady himself as the train rounds a corner. "I've never seen anything like it. I thought you were dead."

I turn my head. My cane's a few feet away. The Birkenstocks woman is eyeing it up. Take it, I want to say, go on, just take it, but I can't seem to speak, and now the man is lifting me to my feet and telling everyone to make room and the train stops and there's a swoosh of the doors and he ushers me across the threshold and onto the platform and we stand looking, me leaning on him, at the train waiting to depart.

"Don't miss it," I say.

"Oh, there'll be another one shortly."

But he wants to get on, I can tell. The doors close and he loses his chance. Instead he guides me to a row of seats, lowering me into the second to last one.

He hands me my cane. "Is there someone I should call?"

From the corner of my eye I see a flash of gold, his wedding ring, thinned by time, tightly wedged into the crease of his chubby digit.

I shake my head. "Not really."

He sits down. "What happened back there?"

"I'm not sure."

Another train pulls up and he tries not to look.

"Go on," I say. "I'm okay now. Thank you so much for your help."

"Someone should stay, make sure you're okay."

"Please, I'm fine."

He hesitates and casts a look of longing at the train.

"Go on, sir. Please."

He gets to his feet. "Well, if you're sure. My wife is waiting for me at home. Take care."

He hurries across the platform and ducks through the doors and stands looking at me through the glass as the train pulls away.

2

"You dropped like a stone."

I think of those words as I emerge from the subway. I'm shocked that it has happened again. I do the math in my head. Five weeks since the last episode. Three months before that. Seven months before that. They are becoming more frequent. I should be getting better by now but I'm only getting worse.

I pause to catch my breath at the top of the subway stairs. Stairs are the worst. Especially steep ones like these. I have to take them one at a time, steady my weight on the cane, haul myself up to the next one, all the while ignoring the pain shooting through my useless semi-foot. That's what they actually call it. A semi-foot. I nearly laughed out loud when I first heard the physical therapist say it during our sessions with the railings.

"That's right, Amelia, lead with your semi-foot."

They like to do that, the helpers, re-label disabilities and items to make them seem like less of a lack. Like my cane. They call it a device. An "assisted living device," to be more precise. Like the word "cane" is somehow derogatory.

Whatever its name, I'm still not used to my cane and the balance it requires. Three years since we were first introduced and I still make rookie mistakes. Like not taking enough care to ensure the rubber stopper at the bottom doesn't slip into a crack. Only last week, I careened face-first into the pavement right outside the courthouse.

Still, there are benefits. No one seems to bother a woman with a cane. If anything, people give me a wide berth because of it, as if I'm blind and they're worried I might walk straight into them. Once someone even tried to give me money.

I carry on to my apartment. I never take the same route home twice in a week. That could mean getting off a different subway stop and then taking a bus, or walking a few blocks (despite the pain), or getting back on the subway, or taking a cab. It's exhausting, constantly being on guard, thinking of the logistics for every journey home. But it's safer that way.

Outside it's as dark as ink and must be close to 1 a.m. And cold. Soon it will be fall. I don't like fall. There are too many reminders in the fall. In the fall I lose my hair. Strands litter the shower floor, stick to the bathroom walls, my pillow, the collar of my black woolen coat. It comes away in my fingers and fills the teeth of my comb. Not clumps exactly, but enough to worry that I might be afflicted with some strange form of seasonal alopecia. Enough to be concerned that the bald patches might never grow back. But they always do. In spring the molting stops and my hair renews. Grayer and more wiry than before. But at least it grows back.

"You dropped like a stone."

I think of myself lying there on the floor of the subway car, people staring at me, the Birkenstocks woman coveting my cane, the husband man helping me. At least there is still one kind soul in the world.

I reach the corner of 13th Street and 3rd Avenue and pause there. I can't decide which route to take. Every route seems risky tonight. The episode on the train has really

152

shaken me. Get a grip, I tell myself, so I choose left and skirt the empty basketball court and cross the road, then double back on the opposite side of the street and head east down 11th and into the alleyway. The alleyway is a narrow access path squeezed between two remodeled tenement buildings. It gives me the creeps but it's well-lit and will bring me out onto the avenue and into the postage stamp playground where I can take cover near the hedgerow to study my apartment building from afar.

I reach the playground and pause at the hedge to look at the building. It's a small eight-story walk-up, red-bricked with iron balconies and fire escape ladders, a former pencil factory converted into apartments back in the 1980s.

I scan the exterior and count four floors up. The new tenant in the floor below has put flowerpots and yucca plants on their balcony. I swear under my breath. Anyone could be hiding there and I wouldn't know it. And from there, they would only need to unclip the fire ladder and climb to my balcony directly above. But there's nothing I can do. People can't stop making their homes look nice just because of me.

There's a sudden movement to the left on the ledge outside the second-story apartment. I tense. Then I see the flick of a tail. It's only the cat, the no-name cat that nobody seems to own. I've seen it before, leaping from one balcony to the next or launching itself from the fire exit ladders to the floors below or above, like some kind of crazy ninja feline. One day that thing's going to slip and tumble headfirst right onto the pavement and its acrobat days will be over.

My eyes shift to my own apartment. The living room lights are on. I look at my watch. Just before two. The lights (two twenty-dollar floor lamps I bought on sale from Home Depot) are set on an automatic timer, and go on and off in pre-scheduled two-hour increments. A ruse so anyone outside would think there was someone home.

The windows are closed and both sets of venetian blinds are the way I left them this morning, hanging down at a precise midway point in the windowpanes, the slats open on a half-inch incline so the internal lights in the apartment shine through to the outside.

I wait there for at least twenty minutes, watching for movement inside the apartment. There's nothing. No one is in there. I am safe.

I emerge from behind the hedgerow and cross the road and head for the building, all the while fighting the urge to return to my hiding place in the playground to check on the apartment again.

It's not the first apartment I have lived in since the incident. There were four more prior to this one. On average I have shifted every six months. To stay ahead. To stay safe. When I have exhausted all the possible combinations of routes I can use to get to an apartment, I know I'm at risk of developing patterns and routines that could be detectable, so the only solution is to move again. Constantly shifting is exhausting and totally at odds with my nature to want to stay in one place. But I do it because there is no real alternative. I'd rather be a moving target than a sitting duck.

I reach the door to my building. It's a push code button type of lock where you key in a combination, but I'm smart enough to know that although this door is meant to be the first line of defense, it's really no defense at all. People can easily slip in behind someone else. Tenants can (and do) give out the code to friends and relatives. So I never trust it. The only real first line of defense is my own apartment door.

Before I key in the code, I glance over my shoulder to study the street. Empty. I slip inside and push the door firmly behind me until I hear the nib click back into place.

The stairwell is to my left. Empty and well-lit. Four flights of stairs are beyond my current capabilities, so I take the elevator instead. An old-fashioned Otis elevator with a scissor gate that no one else bothers to use. It stammers upward to my floor and I walk the six footsteps to my apartment door. I pause and listen as the elevator staggers back down to the ground floor. Someone is playing Xbox in one of the apartments above. A moan of a siren a few streets away.

I push my keys into the dead bolts in my door. There are two of them, state of the art, titanium models. I do not trust potentially corruptible tradesmen so I installed them myself, something I have become very good at from watching YouTube clips.

I unlock the door and stand on the threshold, listening. It's more than listening really. Sensing is a more accurate description, using my gut to get a read on the energy in the apartment, to detect whether someone is in there, invading my territory, filling it up. Tonight there is nothing. But this does not mean I can relax. No way. Now the real work begins.

I'm bone tired and desperate for sleep. I have a full schedule at work tomorrow and need to be on my game. But there's a detailed checking process I must follow before I can even think of going to bed. By now my Home Depot lights are off and I keep it that way. Leaving the front door open, I step inside. Back at the start of all this, after the incident and long stay at the hospital, when I first went to live on my own, when this process of checking began, I faced the dilemma of whether to leave the front door open while I checked the inside of the apartment. A dilemma because someone could sneak through the front door while I was deep in the apartment and carry out a blitz attack on me. But if I locked the door behind me before I checked the rest of the apartment and there *was* someone inside, it would mean I would be trapped in the apartment with them. That's when I came to realize that a good checking strategy was as much about escape as it was about entry. So when I moved here three months ago, the first thing I did was carefully map out the escape routes. Should the worst occur I have three available options:

Flee out my front door. Activate the building's fire alarm on the landing. Bang on everybody's doors. Shout Fire! People come running. Attacker scared off. It's my number one strategy because with my foot how it is, I could never outrun the potential attacker. I could take the elevator, but by the time I got to the ground floor, he would be waiting for me at the bottom of the stairs and I'd be as good as dead.

Climb out the living room window. Get onto the balcony. Unhook the fire escape and make my way down to the next level's balcony and fire escape and so on until I reach the ground. Not easy with my foot but I can do it. One time my neighbor caught me practicing. Mr. Lee from apartment 5b. He's been kind enough to look the other way ever since.

The last resort. Not so much an escape strategy as a final solution. Shoot the fucker in the head with my Glock

156

19 9mm compact semi-automatic pistol that I keep in the side table next to the sofa.

That's it. Only two escape routes out of the apartment, and one last resort, but at least I have a plan.

I cross the living room floor and check that the large window overlooking the balcony is firmly locked, that the venetian blinds have not been touched, that no dust has been stirred. After that, I hang back behind the window frame, look out the window and onto the balcony, and study the dark street below. All clear. I lower the venetian blinds and adjust the slats until they are closed all the way, then walk the circumference of the room, checking that nothing's out of place, that the armchair and sofa have not been sat on or moved.

I head to my bedroom and check the window there. The latch holds firm, the way I left it this morning. The blinds are the same, too. I look around and check that nothing has been moved and it all looks okay. I pause and study my bedroom closet, or what's left of my bedroom closet. I removed the doors when I first came here. The thought of someone hiding inside made me on edge all the time, so I took them off.

It's tidy, with just the bare essentials to aid a clearer view. Everything from my old life is gone. All those frivolous dresses, too short and pretty for me now given my cumbersome foot. Not a high heel in sight, either. Now it's all about sensible orthopedic-adjusted shoes. Serious career pant suits and blazers. Besides, it's easier to get away in flats and trousers than a skirt and kitten heels.

I scan the racks. Two pant suits, one gray, one navy, both with matching blazers. Two neatly pressed white shirts. A beige raincoat and gray knee-length woolen coat complete the collection. Resting on the shoe rack below are two pairs of flats, black and black, and two pairs of Nikes with a special orthopedic insert, my gym bag next to those.

In the three cubby holes to the left, two sweaters and one hoodie sit neat and snug. Below that, a pair of jeans and sweatpants. My workout gear occupies the final cubby.

My eyes scan slowly left to right. It's still dark in there, I think, inside the closet. Despite my attempts at minimalism, I should throw more things out. But not tonight. Tonight I don't have the energy. My eyes reach the winter woolen coat and halt. Oh god, was that movement? Did I hear a breath? Did the hem of my coat shift ever so slightly? My heart begins to race.

I fight the urge to run. Instead, I tell myself to just calm the hell down and take another look. And when I do, I see that I'm wrong. Nothing there except the imaginings of my touchy amygdala. I lower myself onto the bed and take six full breaths to calm my rising panic. No one is there. No one is there. No one is there.

I look at the clock on the bedside table. It's after two. I need to get some sleep or I will be a wreck in the morning. I wonder what my colleagues at the DA's office would think if they could see me now, shaking, out of control, imagining phantoms in the wardrobe.

Heart still pounding, I get up and leave the bedroom. There's nothing to worry about, I tell myself, just finish checking then go to bed. I pause at the door of the spare room next to mine and turn the handle. It does not budge. Still locked. Good.

Next I move to the bathroom, check behind the shower curtain. All clear, so I head back to the front door and turn the knob and check the locks again. Then do the circuit twice more, rechecking the living room, my bedroom, the other room, the bathroom, the front door as thoroughly as I did the first time. Even after I have done the checking three times there is always the urge to check once more.

But I tell myself that everything is fine. The apartment is safe. I am safe. I have done enough for the night. I realize I am shivering. The apartment is freezing. I turn on the heat, twisting the thermostat way up. The crummy thing rattles into life, blows out stale air, but warms the place quickly.

I can barely keep my eyes open and head for my bedroom. A sudden high-pitched beep stops me. My cell phone battery is dying. I turn back and dig inside my purse to put it on the charger. The screen is lit with four missed calls. I listen to them. The first is from my mother. Would Amelia please keep her eye out for the vacation brochure on Bali she'd sent her, and wouldn't it be great if Amelia could meet a nice man to take because she'd heard there were fantastic resorts where you could get couples massages for a very good price. The second message is from Claire Watson, the New Jersey mom of the eleven-year-old child witness I am supposed to be briefing tomorrow. "Amelia? I need to talk to you. Give me a call." Blunt and to the point, in true Claire Watson fashion. Her message was left at 7:38 p.m. It's now nearly 2:30 a.m. Too late to call. It will have to wait until tomorrow. I swallow down the guilt, not sure how I'm going to explain my tardiness. The third is from Lorna. My therapist. She's pissed I missed our appointment. Twice. I look down at the fourth missed call and go cold. Number unknown. No message. It's nothing, I tell myself. I stare at the screen for a long time. It doesn't mean anything, nothing at all. But it's too late, it sets me off and I begin the checking all over again.

Speak for Me (#3 Amelia Kellaway)
By Deborah Rogers

Manipulator. Killer. A time-bomb waiting to explode...

Just weeks away from giving birth, New York prosecutor Amelia Kellaway is about to interview Oregon serial killer, Rex Hawkins, a man who has tormented her for years. Amelia has no other option—Rex insists she be the one to hear his confession otherwise he'll take the details of the string of rapes and murders he's committed to his grave.

Truth be told, Amelia wants to do it. She wants to show Rex Hawkins she's no longer the same person he victimized all those years ago. She's stronger now, braver, smarter and she's determined to get him to tell her everything he knows.

But is Amelia underestimating Rex? What underlies all his talk of redemption and seeking forgiveness? Could he be planning something? And if so, what? As Amelia's due date gets closer and the pressure mounts, events spiral out of control, thrusting both her and Rex onto a devastating final trajectory in which only one of them survives.

About the Author

Deborah Rogers is a psychological thriller and suspense author. Her gripping debut psychological thriller, *The Devil's Wire,* received rave reviews as a "dark and twisted page turner". In addition to standalone novels like *The Devil's Wire* and *Into Thin Air*, Deborah writes the popular Amelia Kellaway series, a gritty suspense series based on New York prosecutor, Amelia Kellaway.

Deborah has a Graduate Diploma in scriptwriting and graduated cum laude from the Hagley Writers' Institute. When she's not writing psychological thrillers and suspense books, she likes to take her chocolate Lab, Rocky, for walks on the beach and make decadent desserts.

www.deborahrogersauthor.com